R

A
PERSISTENT
ECHO

BRIAN KAUFMAN

Black Rose Writing | Texas

The author grants the final approval for this literary material.

First printing

This is a work of fiction. Names, characters, businesses, places, events, and incidents are either the products of the author's imagination or used in a fictitious manner. Any resemblance to actual persons, living or dead, or actual events is purely coincidental.

ISBN: 978-1-68513-262-0 (Paperback); 978-1-68513-268-2 (Hardcover)
PUBLISHED BY BLACK ROSE WRITING
www.blackrosewriting.com

Printed in the United States of America
Suggested Retail Price (SRP) $20.95 (Paperback); $25.95 (Hardcover)

A Persistent Echo is printed in Baskerville

*As a planet-friendly publisher, Black Rose Writing does its best to eliminate unnecessary waste to reduce paper usage and energy costs, while never compromising the reading experience. As a result, the final word count vs. page count may not meet common expectations.

PRAISE FOR
A
PERSISTENT
ECHO

"Kaufman is a fantastic writer with a distinctive poetic touch... It will be the rare reader who will not be moved by this soulful, poignant novel."

–Kirkus Reviews

"It's a powerfully-rendered novel that holds the rare ability to traverse genres to attract a wider audience of reader than the 'historical fiction' label portends."

–Midwest Book Review

"This heartfelt story, filled with wit and wisdom, kept me reading late into the night and waking eager for the next page. August Simms, Kaufman's protagonist, will stay with me."

–Linda Rosen, author of Sisters of the Vine

"...a page-turner with a captivating storyline. (4 out of 4 stars!)"

–Online Book Club

"Brian Kaufman has woven a tale of friendship, betrayal, and hope. His descriptions of setting and mood are spot on... highly recommended."

–Karen Brees, author of Crosswind

To Gus, sorely missed.

A
PERSISTENT
ECHO

"How strange this fear of death is!
We are never frightened at a sunset."
~George MacDonald

"History is a gallery of pictures in which there are
few originals and many copies."
~Alexis de Tocqueville

"Maybe all one can do is hope to end up with the right regrets."
~Arthur Miller

CHAPTER ONE

Rhome, Texas
Saturday, April 17, 1897

As the train lurches to a stop, August Simms awakens. He is upright in the Pullman car, his shoulder pressed against the wooden window frame. The seat next to him, formerly occupied by the businessman from Dallas, is empty. The cloth blinds are pulled down, so August raises them and peers outside. Like images in a tintype, the sun, the train station, the vegetation beyond the platform, and the dusty sky appear in shades of yellow and brown. Rhome, Texas. He has arrived.

The businessman, a portly gentleman smelling of cigars and whiskey, had disembarked without a proper goodbye—a relief. They'd gone crossways when the man repeatedly called the porter "George," a reference to the owner of the Pullman company. Worse, the man snored like a cannon barrage.

August grabs the top of the seat in front of him and pulls himself up, pausing to steady his legs. Sitting too long is not good for his circulation. His hips ache, and his head swims in the heat. Sweat crawls down his shoulders and nestles in the small of his back.

When he is sure of his balance, August makes his way to the front of the car. The porter, who worked through the night, stands at the door, grinning like an old Cheshire cat. One of his incisors is missing. He touches the brim of his cap. "We here, Suh."

The two men clasp hands, and the gold coin that was in August's palm is now in the porter's.

"Thank you, Isaac. Will you be moving on with the train?"

"Riding on into Fort Worth."

August smiles. "You hug that daughter of yours for me. Tell her I enjoyed hearing her adventures."

"I will. It'll be good to be home."

August squints into the sun through the open door. "Home." He sighs. "I suppose this is home for me."

"Well, then. Welcome home, Suh."

August steps from the train onto the platform. The porter holds his elbow, steadying him.

"Thank you, Isaac."

Three steps onto the platform, the heat strikes him like a caulking mallet. "It's only April," he whispers. He remembers cool evenings on the Martins' porch with his wife, Christy, and hopes the memories don't lie.

A moment later, Isaac delivers his leather and canvas trunk, wiping the brass locks with his shirt sleeve. "Is someone meetin' you here?" he asks.

"No," August says. "But don't you worry. I know my way around. There's a boarding house just up the road, and as soon as I've got my feet under me, I'll be on my way."

Isaac's smile disappears. "The train's leaving, else I'd carry this here trunk for you."

"You're a good man, Isaac."

"I was gonna say the same 'bout you." The porter squints, and there's gravel in his voice. "You take care, Mister Simms."

August smiles and looks away. At his age, nearly every goodbye is a last goodbye. Though he's had practice, he will never acquire grace or skill in the art of parting ways.

Alone again, August sniffs the hot air. The locomotive stinks of coal and oil.

He'd boarded the train in Folsom, New Mexico, riding the "Denver Road" into Texas. He has traveled all his life, as far east as Russian Armenia and as far west as the Solomon Islands. Today, his hips and back tell him that his traveling days are at an end. He sits on his trunk and watches the locomotive pull out of the station. Eventually, he'll lug the trunk down the road, unless someone kind comes by with a wagon.

The sun overhead says noon. There's a watch on a fob in his pocket, but he's loath to pull it out and confirm what he already knows. He recalls the businessman's rumbling snore. He recalls the ornate ceiling of the Pullman car, wishing he'd had another hour of sleep before being popped like a Texas biscuit into this oven of a train station.

When he is ready, he gathers himself for a walk. The heavy trunk would have been less so, but he'd packed treasured books— the five he could not do without—along with a handful of souvenirs, including a fragment from an eight-pounder, lava rock from the mountain in Armenia, and the large brass compass from a submarine.

He does not have a desk, he thinks, but he has paperweights.

August pulls the bag along, pausing to rest just outside the entrance to the train station. There, a man sits watching from his wagon. He wears bib overalls without a shirt, which seems prudent, given the heat. His age is hard to determine. He has a young face, but his skin is like tanned hide. "Hello there, old timer," he calls. "That trunk o' yours looks heavy."

"Looks are not deceiving."

"Somebody coming by to help you with that?"

"No, sir. I am left to my own devices."

"Exactly where is that trunk heading?" The hint of a smile tugs at the corners of the man's mouth.

"Does the Martin family still run a boarding house?"

"You mean Nadine? She sure does." He sits back and points down the road. "Half mile this way. Long ways for a trunk." His gaze narrows. "I might be convinced to give you a ride."

"Convinced, eh? Are you looking for a compelling argument?"

The man snorts. "I am notoriously hard to persuade. I guess I'd be satisfied with a please and thank you." He hops down from the flatbed wagon, pats his horse's flank, and climbs the steps. "With your permission?"

"Please," August says, grinning. He holds out a hand. "Name's August Simms."

"Simms?" the man asks as he gives the hand a vigorous shake. "Bill Ackerman." The trunk secured, he points at the passenger side of the wagon. "Need help getting up in the seat?"

August rounds the wagon and looks. "I can manage," he says.

A minute later, Ackerman has the wagon rolling. The horse's pace is one step faster than a crawl, but August is not in a hurry. Ackerman chews on his lip, occasionally calling out to the horse for no apparent reason, leaving August to his own thoughts. He watches the roadside vegetation creep by as they travel. Cheatgrass, side oats, and heartleaf nettles battle each other for moisture from the ground. A motte of oaks in the distance breaks the dusty horizon. A mosquito lands on August's hand and then flies off. *Slim pickings for the insects,* he thinks.

Ackerman points. "There's the house. Nadine will likely be glad to see you. Not a lot of visitors these days."

"Is the flour mill still running?"

Ackerman glances at him. "Two of 'em. The new one's a fancy roller mill. Makes white flour." He bites his lip again. "You from here? You sound Yankee."

August nods. "Born in Ohio. But I stayed here for the summer years ago. For the most part, it was a happy time."

"What brings you back?"

"I read about the flying machine in the papers and became curious."

The first reports of a flying machine had surfaced in California and the Midwest. Incidents in Texas had begun just days earlier. Witnesses told of a mysterious craft, anywhere from fifty to a hundred feet long, bearing a searchlight and unknown weaponry. The morning newspaper in Folsom referenced sightings in Rhome, a place August knew very well. He'd packed his trunk and boarded the Fort Worth and Denver City Railway that afternoon.

Ackerman snorts and bites his lip. "You ain't one of them airship chasers, are you?"

August considers before answering. "Perhaps I am. But my curiosity is inspired by a love of science and a desire to see a miracle."

"A miracle?" Ackerman repeats, pulling on the reins to stop the horse. The wagon goes from slow to stop. "Well, here's one for you—we got here before dark."

August chuckles. He likes this man's sense of humor. "You haven't seen the airship yourself?"

Ackerman snorts again. "No sir. A lot of people in town claim to have seen it, though. You buy a round down at Hanson's, and you'll hear all the stories you want."

"Hanson's?"

"Hanson's Mercantile. General store, hardware, and distillery. When old men retire from the mills, they go there to play Whist and drink." He hops down from the wagon and begins tugging at the trunk. "You carry a body in here?"

"Body of work," August says.

Ackerman stifles a laugh. He places the trunk beside the wagon and says, "Well, I guess I'll be going. Places to be."

August reaches for his pocket, but Ackerman waves him off. "If you do go down to Hanson's, there's a good chance you'll find me. My wagon ends up there of its own accord. I'll be pleased to have you buy me a drink."

August nods. "That is a promise. Thank you."

Their arrival has drawn the attention of the proprietor. She is a handsome woman in her thirties, wearing a plain dress and apron. "Hello, Nadine," Ackerman calls as he turns his wagon around. He does not stop to chat.

Nadine frowns from the front porch. Her dark hair is tied behind her in a loose bundle, but strands fall in front of her face. Her shoulders are slumped. She rubs her eyes and then closes them. "How long are you staying?"

There is no sign that she has recognized him. "I'll be here for several weeks at least. Do you have a room for me?"

"Thirty dollars a week, paid in advance. Meals at seven, noon, and five. Be on time or fend for yourself." Her voice is stern, but there is a hint of something else there, like the smell of sandalwood in a summer breeze.

August tugs at his trim white beard. "Very reasonable. If it's acceptable, I'll pay you for a month in advance."

She can't keep the surprise from her face. He decides that the money is an unexpected boon. Good. He reaches for the gold coins he pocketed for the trip.

"No cooking in the rooms. The bathroom has plumbing. Keep your personals in your room."

"Understood," he says, extending his handful of coins.

"Doors are locked at ten. No company at unseasonable hours."

August laughs. "I'm at the end of my season, I'm afraid."

Nadine blushes. She hasn't taken the money. "The common areas include the dining room, sitting room, and the porch. No furniture in the rooms without permission."

August points with his coin hand at the travel trunk behind him. "That's all I have. That's everything."

She exhales and takes his money, stuffing it into the pocket of her apron. August retrieves the trunk and pulls it toward the porch steps. The house is much as he remembered it, though time has whittled it down, just as time has worked its malevolent magic on him. Gutters droop. Shingles are missing on the roof. The porch, which wraps around the house to the right, has a damaged rail and slats. The bay window to the right of the porch steps is bordered by a recent coat of white paint. The rest of the house is a faded yellow.

"Can you manage?" she asks, gesturing at his trunk.

"Yes," he says. "I wonder if I might inquire, is the downstairs room to the right available?"

Again, surprise without recognition. "You've stayed here before, then?"

"Yes," he says. "In 1882."

Nadine walks him past the front door, through the sitting room and down the hall. "That room is available. For the best, I suppose. I don't want you tumbling down the stairs in the middle of the night." She pauses, perhaps to frown at him, or maybe to allow him and his trunk to catch up. "What's your name?"

"August Simms, at your service. And yours?"

"Nadine Martin," she says. "Call me Nadine. We are informal here in the house."

Martin. Her parents' name. Did she never marry?

The room in question has not changed. A bed, a chest of drawers, a tiny desk and chair. The large window facing northeast looks out over the end of the wraparound veranda. This room is cooler than the rest of the house. August is relieved that he'd recalled that much correctly.

He turns to the bed. A new quilted bedspread, but the same old frame. The same four posts. He puts a hand on one of the polished finials to steady himself. His legs tremble. For a moment, he closes his eyes. He can almost smell his wife's hair. August opens his eyes again, blinking back the memory.

Nadine does not notice. She runs a finger across the top of the desk, looking for dust. There isn't any. The room is immaculate. "My mother was the innkeeper when you stayed here?"

"Both your father and mother."

She does not flinch. "That was a long time ago."

"Yes," he agrees, setting his trunk against the wall. He straightens, squaring his shoulders. "Your father was a fine man."

A voice from behind interrupts them. A girl, a teen by appearances, steps into the doorway. She wears a blue pastel shirtwaist and a skirt that is grass-stained at the hem. Twisting in place, she tugs at what August assumes is a corset. She has a lovely face—a perfect oval with large green eyes. Her lips press into a thin, irritated line.

"Hello," August says. He turns to Nadine. "Is this your daughter? The resemblance is striking."

The girl scowls.

"Natalie, say hello to Mr. Simms."

"I didn't finish in the shed. I'll finish tomorrow."

Nadine smiles, showing her teeth. August takes an involuntary step back. "Say hello to Mr. Simms, Natalie," she repeats.

"*Hello.*" The girl lifts her chin and scowls.

August muses that if Charon the ferryman greeted the souls crossing the river Styx, he would use that very tone of voice. Nevertheless, he bows and says, "I am pleased to meet you."

"Now, go back to the shed," Nadine commands. "You'll finish the job today."

CHAPTER TWO

Martins' Boarding house
Saturday, April 17, 1897

The evening meal is served promptly at five. The table sits in the center of the kitchen. Both the old dining room and the parlor have been converted to rooms. Nadine and her daughter Natalie set serving plates at the center of the table. Biscuits, fresh from the oven, and pickled beans, the last of the winter stores, accompany the roast pork. Having lived in similar places for many years, August is familiar with the "boarding house reach"—the scramble for the best cuts of meat and a fair portion share. He lets the others at the table fill their plates before taking a biscuit and a small piece of pork.

"You have to be quicker than that," the man to his right says. William Chambers is a short, stout man who uses a cane to get to and from the dining table. He sports a salt-and-pepper goatee that extends to the top of his chest. He is losing his hair on top, something everyone can see because of his diminutive stature. His stomach acts as a shelf for his hands, which rest with fingers interlaced when he is not eating, though he is eating now, diving into a plate piled high with biscuits and pork, along with a tablespoon or two of vegetable.

"Mr. Simms?" Nadine asks. "Do you have enough to eat?"

"I do," August says.

"Simms?" Chambers asks, as if chewing on the name instead of the biscuit in his hand. "I know that we were introduced, but I didn't catch your first name."

"August."

Chambers swallows. "August Simms. I believe I know of an August Simms. Explorer of sorts."

August cuts his biscuit in half and stuffs the pork slice inside. He takes a bite. The flavor is surprisingly good. He glances at Nadine. "This is marvelous. What is the seasoning?"

"Coriander," Nadine says. Her eyes go wide.

"Yes, quite delicious," Chambers says. "One of your better meals."

"Pleased to hear it," Nadine says, glaring at Chambers. "Must be extraordinary for you to take notice."

"When something's good, proper acknowledgement should be made," Chambers says. He fingers his goatee, smiling. Across the table, young Natalie rolls her eyes.

Chambers pats his lips with a napkin and adds, "Coriander seeds grow wild in Portugal." He turns to August. "In your travels, have you encountered the seeds?"

"Coriander grows wild in the Land of Israel as well."

"Ah. The Levant." Chambers nods. He pats his lips again. "You may not be aware, but the spice's name comes from the Greek word *koris*—the stink bug. It refers to the peculiar odor."

Nadine is bent over the table, retrieving the empty serving platter. "Oh, my. I hope the odor doesn't bother you." Her expression says something entirely different.

Young Natalie puts down her fork, sighing. She pinches the bridge of her nose with her thumb and index finger. She is the only person in the room under the age of thirty, and she looks as if she'd rather be anywhere else. *Perhaps Portugal or Israel*, August thinks.

Also seated at the table are Thomas MacGregor and Richard Allen. Both men eat silently, paying little attention to either Chambers or the women in the room.

MacGregor had been introduced as an old Indian fighter. He sports a full mustache that extends downward beyond his jaw, frayed and bushy at the ends. His long gray hair is pulled back, reaching down to his shoulders. The small finger on his right hand is missing, gone at the first joint.

Richard Allen is the pastor of the local Methodist church. As such, he opened the meal with a terse prayer. Now that the meal has ended, he sits with both arms propped against the table's edge, fingers steepled.

Nadine taps her daughter on the shoulder. Natalie stands with a frown and begins collecting empty plates.

Chambers burps and pats his stomach affectionately. "The August Simms I'm thinking of traveled to the eastern portion of the world back in the forties. Went climbing in the mountains described in the Bible."

With this, Pastor Allen takes notice. He is a thin man with a prominent jaw. His clothing is plain, in keeping with the Methodist rejection of ruffles, colored shirts, and other costly embellishments. His sole ornament is a shock of brown hair that he keeps oiled and parted in the center. He leans forward, a serious look on his face. "Seven mountains are mentioned in scripture. Which mountain did you visit?"

This is a discussion August would prefer to avoid, and a truthful answer will certainly lead to more questions. However, he will not deny a direct question. "Ararat."

Pastor Allen sits back, his mouth open, as if flabbergasted. Chambers looks at the pastor and smiles. "That's what I remembered."

"Why would you climb Ararat?" the pastor asks. His chin juts out like the cowcatcher on a locomotive. He seems almost angry.

"The mountain has interesting volcanic features," August says. He could stop there, but to do so would be a lie of omission— something he will not allow. "There is, of course, the archeological significance of the area."

"That is what I remembered," Chambers repeats.

Pastor Allen clears his throat. *"He shall not enter into the holy place inside the veil before the mercy seat which is on the ark. Leviticus 16:2."*

August forces a smile. "I believe the scripture refers to the Ark of the Covenant."

Pastor Allen's gaze narrows.

"Nevertheless," August continues, "the wisdom applies. One must act with care and reverence in everything one does. That is a principle I adhered to in my travels east."

The pastor's expression relaxes, his jaw receding until it is nearly in alignment with his upper jaw.

"You went to Ararat," Nadine says. It is a statement, rather than a question.

"Yes." He meets her gaze. "I am eighty-six years old. When one lives that long, the list of places visited and things accomplished gives the illusion of constant activity. In truth, most of my life has been quite ordinary."

"I've never been *anywhere*," Natalie says as she stacks plates in the sink. Now that the evening meal has concluded, her chores have begun again.

"Where would you like to travel?" August asks.

Natalie turns from the sink. "Anywhere. Anywhere but Texas."

August smiles. "There are worse places."

"Far worse," MacGregor says. This is the first time he's spoken. Given the look on Nadine's face, MacGregor has surprised her by joining the conversation.

Chambers appears pleased by MacGregor's words. "Well, sir," he says. "I would be curious as to what the worst place you've seen might be. I have my own answer, of course, but I'd be pleased to hear yours."

MacGregor looks at August, rather than the others. "The Palo Duro Canyon," he says, his voice laced with a thick Scottish brogue. "Aye, we attacked the camps of the Comanche. Dinnae find them, so we killed their ponies. Colonel Mackenzie gave the order. The man's heart was as black as the Earl of Hell's waistcoat." He turns to Natalie. "Ye widnae want to see a field of dead ponies. Be happy. Texas is a paradise."

"A horrible thing to witness," August says.

"And you, sir?" MacGregor says, eyes narrowed. "You fought in the War of Secession?"

"I did," August answers, surprised.

Nadine sits down in a chair near the stove, away from the table, hands in her lap.

"You must have seen terrible things as well," Chambers says.

August nods. "Certainly not a topic for the dining table." He shifts his chair, facing MacGregor. "I would be very interested in your recollections. Perhaps later, on the veranda. I did not take up arms against the Indian nations, and I know little enough about such things. Your experiences would be instructive." August brushes at his face with his fingers, aware that crumbs cling to the lips of old men, undetected. "I wonder, sir, how you knew I fought in the War Between the States."

MacGregor's old face carries traces of a smile. "Perhaps you carry yourself like an army man. Confident, but cautious? You search the room with your eyes before sitting. And ye dinnae have the *gallus*"—he pauses to glance at Chambers— "common to North Texas."

"An interesting word. In the German Empire, it means *stranger*," August says. He smiles at Nadine, and then returns his attention to MacGregor. "Where in Caledonia are you from?"

MacGregor's eyes widen. "You read poetry, sir?"

August nods. He's used a romantic, lyrical name for Scotland, and now he knows that MacGregor is well read. He will enjoy conversing with the man. The Scot is small to have been an Indian fighter, but then, Kit Carson was barely five feet tall. MacGregor is in his fifties, or perhaps early sixties. His face is creased with permanent frown lines, as if his experiences have dry-gulched him.

"I hail from auld Edinburgh. Have ye been there as well?"

"Once," August says. "A beautiful, old-world city." He turns to Pastor Allen. "And you, sir? Where have your travels taken you?"

The pastor clears his throat. "When I was young, the urge to roam was strong. Instead, I stayed here in Rhome to tend to the needs of the flock. *The heart of man plans his way, but the Lord establishes his steps.* Proverbs 16:9."

"The town is lucky to have you," August says.

"But surely, you'd have wanted to see the world?" Chambers asks. "The Holy Land, perhaps?" He lays a hand on August's shoulder. "I venture to say that this man has seen things that would offer great meaning to a man of the cloth."

"My faith gives me vision enough."

August looks to Natalie, who leans against a sink full of dishes, listening. "What about you, young lady? If you could travel anywhere, what would be your first destination?"

Natalie stands frozen in place, as if contemplating such a wish leaves her unable to decide. "I don't know," she says.

"You're young. You've time to consider." August smiles at her. She turns away, back to her chores.

"When I was her age, I knew exactly what I wanted to do with my life," Chambers says.

"How, then, did ye end up here?" MacGregor asks. Chambers flinches.

"Providence has its plan for each of us," Nadine says, standing. "It's a blessing for me and mine that you were all sent here to dine with us."

Now, it's the men's turn to be surprised. August surmises that she is usually a silent presence. Women are not always welcome participants in the discourse of men. *But this is her house,* August thinks. *And I believe she's a woman with something to say.*

"I'm away for a *dauner*," MacGregor says. He scoots his chair back. "Shall we talk more later?"

"Yes, indeed. Enjoy your walk, then," August says.

Pastor Allen rises and leaves without a word, but August finds him a brusque, distant sort, so he does not worry over the absence of a goodbye.

As Chambers stands, cane propping his stance, he says, "It was most pleasing to have mealtime conversation. I look forward to sharing my experiences with you as well."

August agrees with a happy smile. When Chambers is gone, Nadine says, "Your presence was a stimulant, sir. We've not had so many words spoken at the table before."

"I hope it was not an annoyance."

"Not at all. I'd once imagined mealtime in a boarding house to be a close cousin to a salon. For Texas, I mean. This evening was a welcome exception to the usual silence."

Natalie mutters something.

"Speak up," Nadine says.

"I said, no surprise. Men like to chew the fat."

"You're being disrespectful."

"Disrespectful, perhaps, but accurate," August says. He uses the table for balance as he stands. "I was grateful for your contribution to the discussion," he tells Natalie.

Nadine lifts an eyebrow, glancing at her daughter and then back at August. "Some men think that children should be seen, not heard."

"Your daughter has a mind and is willing to speak it. Much like her mother."

Natalie squints. "You talk funny."

August chuckles. "We all have our foibles and embellishments. Like Mr. MacGregor's brogue." He steps away from the table, having gotten his legs underneath him. "Thank you for a fine meal."

Nadine frowns. "You didn't eat much."

"Enough to both sustain and enjoy," he says.

"You are very thin."

"An advantage in the heat, I assure you. Now, I must ask you a question."

"Yes?" There is apprehension in her voice.

"I should like to go to and from the boarding house to various nearby locations. Can you suggest a means?"

"You came here in Ackerman's wagon. He's a likely candidate."

"My plans require venturing out during the work week."

She snorts—a most surprising sound. August is charmed. "Ackerman doesn't *work*," she says, laughing. "He rides around in that damned wagon of his all day."

"Well, then. Perhaps he'll listen to a proposition."

She frowns again. Deeper, this time.

She does not know what to think of me, August decides. Good sense on her part. An elderly man shows up in Rhome, Texas carrying a trunk as large as he is. He is familiar with the boarding house but offers no explanation.

She was a clever child, and by all appearances, she's a clever woman. Kept the boarding house running and raised her child alone, no husband in sight. She may eventually recognize August. Or not. Either way, she will know him for the kind of man he is. If she is amenable, he will stay here in the boarding house until his business is finished.

CHAPTER THREE

Prairie Point Schoolhouse
Sunday, April 18, 1897

August awakens after a restless night. He'd gone to bed hoping, against all reason, that he might sense his wife's presence in the room. Instead, he passed the hours staring at the ceiling—an annoying habit—waiting for morning. Now, aching, he takes a portion of medicine from his travel trunk and dresses. His left arm is mostly useless. Unable to negotiate the sleeve of his shirt, it takes him longer than expected to ready himself for breakfast.

The other boarders are already at the dining table. Morning sun shines against the butter-colored walls. The kitchen smells of warm bread.

Nadine sets a plate of biscuits next to an open jar of jam, followed by a platter with scrambled eggs and sausages. A pitcher of lemonade rounds out the meal. Sunday breakfasts are more elaborate than the rest of the week, but today's breakfast is special, because it is Easter morning. August recalls a time when he might have filled his plate, but today, the sight of so much food does not entice him. He takes a single biscuit and a spoon of apricot jam.

William Chambers is holding court on the topic of the airship sightings. MacGregor is listening, perhaps, but Pastor Allen seems immersed in his own thoughts. He will deliver a sermon later in the morning. August is told that services are held at the Prairie Point

Schoolhouse. The weather seems to have relented, so the indoor service will not be oppressive.

Natalie sits at the table with the men while her mother finishes serving. The young girl appears to be in a good mood. The talk of airships seems to capture her interest.

"I'm told on good authority," Chambers says, "that the airship is able to attain speeds of more than a hundred miles per hour."

"How do they know?" Natalie asks, half a biscuit in her mouth.

"There are men who are experts in such matters," Chambers assures her.

August thinks that Nadine's biscuits are delicious.

"What is your opinion of the airship, sir?" Chambers asks.

August puts his biscuit down on the small plate and swallows what's in his mouth before speaking. "I came to Rhome, in part, to satisfy my curiosity about the matter."

Nadine, standing at the sink, frowns as if she disapproves.

"Your opinion?" Chambers repeats.

August smiles. "I haven't formed one."

"Surely, you must have an inkling?"

"None at all," August says. "The idea that so many sightings of a similar nature have occurred in so many different locations is intriguing. I look forward to interviewing some of the witnesses."

"Are you with the press, then?" MacGregor asks.

"No," August says. "I'm an honest man."

MacGregor laughs.

Chambers appears undeterred. "But your curiosity itself would indicate that you find possibility in the existence of such a ship."

"Or ships. Multiple sightings in different places at the same time. A large number of witnesses."

"Ah, they're all *dighted*," MacGregor says.

"I'm not so sure. There are elements of the story that give one pause." August takes another bite of his biscuit. The jam is thick, tart, and sweet.

"Will you be attending services?" Pastor Allen asks, suddenly attentive.

"I should like to. How is everyone getting to the service?"

"The schoolhouse isn't far," MacGregor says. "We walk."

"I shall join you, then."

"I'm afraid I won't be able to attend," Chambers says. He scoots his chair back and taps his knee, as if presenting the only explanation necessary.

"It has been a while since you last worshipped," Pastor Allen says.

"It has been a while since I was able to walk without my friend, here." Chambers taps the head of his cane. "What will today's sermon entail? The usual Easter message?"

The pastor clears his throat. *"And I will grant wonders in the sky above, and signs on the earth below. Blood and fire, and vapor of smoke.* Acts 2:19."

"The flying craft?" Chambers asks.

The pastor purses his lips. "All that happens on earth and in heaven fall under His watchful eye. *The thing that hath been, it is that which shall be.*"

"Ecclesiastes?" August asks.

"Yes," the pastor says, a smile threatening the corners of his mouth.

"You must have an opinion on the flying craft, Pastor." Chambers presses on. "What is the church's position on the sightings?"

Pastor Allen grunts and scoots his chair back, scraping the wood floor beneath him. "You should attend the service, sir." He stands, patting his hair in place.

"Could the lights be angels, then?" Chambers asks. He is smiling.

Pastor Allen scowls and leaves the room.

. . .

The sun, so friendly during breakfast, has begun to scorch the road. August brushes at his upper lip. His goatee, white as Galveston sand, is soaked ten minutes into the walk.

"Are ye well?" MacGregor asks.

"I'm well, thank you," August says. He is moving faster than he'd like, but everyone in the group is younger. He must keep up. Natalie, the youngest of them all, is far ahead of the rest, bouncing over the dirt road as if hips, ankles, and knees lasted forever.

Ahead, the sound of hymns drifts over the open field. "Is that the church?" August asks.

"No," MacGregor says. "That's where the negroes worship."

"They're Methodists, too," Natalie calls back.

"Well then," August says, hiding a smile.

Closer now, he can hear the music better. Lovely voices.

"And you, sir?" August asks MacGregor. "Are you Methodist as well?"

MacGregor snorts. "When I was a lad, I attended the Free Church of Scotland."

"Not a Methodist, then?"

MacGregor shakes his head. "Aye, but I give the pastor a listen. Better than staying behind with that *numptie*."

"You don't seem to like Mr. Chambers."

"I like him well enough when he's silent." MacGregor stops and eyes August. "How long were ye in Alba?"

"One spring."

MacGregor nods, seemingly lost in thought. He's sweating, and he pats the ends of his unruly mustache. At last, he says, "I knew you for a soldier, and it dinnae have anything to do with the way ye looked about the room." After a few steps more, he says, "I heard your name before."

August frowns.

"Makes no never mind to me," MacGregor says.

"You fought for the South?"

"Aye," MacGregor says. "But that war is over."

"A new one coming, I'm afraid," August says.

"Aye."

The road is now little more than a path through switchgrass. The air smells of rich soil and sweet greenery with a hint of spice. When the morning breeze shifts, the smell of manure slides in from the west. Later, when the sun reaches its apex, the odor will intensify. Texas is cattle country.

MacGregor taps August's shoulder and points. Pastor Allen strides ahead, arms swinging. "He's working the bellows. He'll have a fiery sermon for us, judging by his walk."

"How is he as a speaker?"

MacGregor spits. "A fine show. If you dinnae like the words, ye can watch his arms wave."

"You are not a spiritual man, MacGregor?"

"I call on God when the bullets fly, same as any man."

"Amen," August says.

Ahead, past a huge elm tree, the Prairie Point Schoolhouse sits nestled in the switchgrass. The entrance is graced with four narrow wood columns and a porch that rises six inches off the ground. The building had once been red—a fact that a subsequent coat of whitewash fails to hide. Most of the congregation is clustered in the yard, waiting until the last moment to go inside. Ackerman is near the entrance. He's watching Nadine. She crooks a finger at him and he ambles over.

"Good Sunday," he says. He is addressing them all, but his eyes are on Nadine.

"Bill," she says. Her voice is both sweet and sour, and she has his full attention. "You remember Mr. Simms?"

"A day's gone by, but yes, I remember him."

"Mr. Simms is in need of transportation," she says. "You have a wagon." She gives August a glance. "I'll leave you to discuss the details." Having made her point, she walks to the schoolhouse entrance and steps inside.

Ackerman watches her walk away. "Where am I driving you to?"

August smiles. "She's a handsome woman, isn't she?"

Ackerman's jaw moves side to side, as if he's grinding his teeth.

"I am interested in the flying machine," August says. "For curiosity's sake, I would like to talk to some of the people I've read about in the papers."

Ackerman scratches his chin. "Well, I guess we can do that. Who do you want to talk to first?"

"I have a list."

Ackerman is looking at him, head tilted, giving him a better peripheral view of the school entrance. "Sounds like thirsty work. We can lunch at Hanson's."

"Of course. I'm buying."

"Then I'm having lunch. From a Mason jar, most probably." He turns to his right and calls, "Nute Rivers!"

Twenty feet away, a wizened old man turns, balancing his pivot on a cane. August measures himself against the man and finds him smaller, frailer, and nearly as old. He is dressed in a worn brown suit with far too much wool for a hot day. He does not seem to mind. Wisps of white hair top his weathered pate.

Ackerman leads August to the old man. "Nute Rivers, this here is August Simms. He came here from parts unknown to talk to people who saw the flying machine. I told him you were a man of substance who can answer his questions."

Nute squints at August, though the sun is behind him. "You a newspaper man?" he asks. "Fort Worth?"

"No." August does not add his usual joke about honesty and hard work. This man strikes him as a no-nonsense sort.

"Good. Might have had to hit you with my cane." His expression is solemn as a pipe organ.

Ackerman smiles. "Nute feels like the local papers did him wrong."

Nute grimaces. "The reporter was a regular Mickey Dugan. Yellow as yellow gets. Made up half of what he wrote."

"Who's Mickey Dugan?" August asks.

"A cartoon character in the New York papers," Ackerman says. August decides that Ackerman will be a useful interpreter of the locals.

"What did the reporter get wrong?"

"Windows," Nute says, spitting the word out as if his mouth had been full of chew. "I told them the thing was the size of a Pullman, so they gave it windows. There weren't no damned windows."

"Big as a Pullman, you say?"

"Maybe. Maybe a little bigger." He pauses. His gaze slips to the side, where a gaggle of townspeople are watching, hands covering their smiles. He scowls. "He got the speed wrong, too."

"How so?"

"Paper said the thing was moving 150 miles an hour. Said we watched it for five minutes." Nute squints again. "Something moving that fast ain't gonna stay in view for no five minutes."

"How fast did it move?" August has a faint smile on his face. He likes this man.

"How the hell would I know that?" Nute says. "I told them the thing was moving fast, but I didn't say no speed."

"Well," August says. "I have a good idea of what the craft wasn't. Can you tell me what it was?"

"No damned idea. It was dark, and the spotlight near the front of the thing was bright. Bright as a lighthouse lamp. Hurt my eyes."

"Bright as a locomotive headlight?"

"Brighter. And the beam moved."

As August considers this, the crowd outside heads toward the schoolhouse door. The service will begin soon. "How high off the ground? Could you tell?"

Nute Rivers shrugs. "Twenty, maybe thirty feet. Not high."

"Was anyone else with you?"

"Oh, yes. Elmer Helm stood about as close to me as you are now. There were others that saw the thing, too."

"When did you lose sight of it?"

"The moment I turned my back."

"Pardon?"

Nute shivers. The Texas sun is high enough to do its damage, and he's wearing a suit. The man is not shivering from the weather. "I turned my back," he repeated. "Elmer and me ran like hell." He taps his cane on the grass. "Fast as this damned thing would allow."

August waits, his head tilted. A question.

"It flew low to the ground," Nute explains. "Searchlight panning left and right. Don't know who or what that thing was, but I know what it was doing." He sniffs. "It was *hunting.*"

August feels a tiny shiver of his own.

"Well," Nute says. "Service is about to begin. Feels like if I miss so much as a single word, it makes the Devil smile." He starts toward the school entrance, his cane leading the way.

As he passes, August touches his sleeve. "Thank you for talking to me."

Nute pauses. This close, August can see that his eyes are a bit rheumy. Nute says, "You know how to listen. Simms, was it?"

"August Simms. Hope to talk to you again soon."

"You will," Ackerman says when Nute is gone. "We'll be at Hanson's later on today."

CHAPTER FOUR

Hanson's Mercantile
Sunday, April 18, 1897

The church service is predictably impassioned. Nearly every white man and woman in town have jammed themselves into the tiny schoolhouse. The women fan themselves and the men drip sweat into their laps. When the pastor's dire warnings have been dispensed, he concludes with a more conventional Easter message of hope, rebirth, and resurrection.

Afterward, the flock makes its way into the yard for fresh air and gossip. Several of the townspeople introduce themselves, and August greets them all with a smile, even stopping to explain the difference between fire and brimstone to an older widow. "Brimstone is an old name for sulphur," he says. "When heated, it gives off an odor like rotten eggs."

"Hell offers plenty of both," the woman assures him.

Having passed the initial scrutiny, August climbs into Ackerman's wagon, and together, they head down the road to Hanson's Mercantile.

The old country store looks run down from the outside. The roof over the porch sags, and the storefront might not have seen fresh paint since Sam Houston died. The inside, however, is swept and dusted. August smells coffee and tobacco, fresh berries and peppermint. To the right, four aisles of goods, from clothing to building supplies. To the left, four small tables and a number of chairs—only one occupied.

"Nute Rivers beat us here," Ackerman says.

"Impossible," August says. "How could he outrun Apollo's chariot?"

Ackerman gives him the kind of slow, lazy grin that demands a blade of grass to chew on. "You are a funny man, August Simms."

James Hanson stands behind a counter at the center of the store. Behind the counter, glass jars full of candies. "Did you come to settle your tab?" he asks Ackerman.

"It's the eighteenth. Twelve more days before Judgement," Ackerman says. "I will take a cup of your world-famous coffee, though. I'm building an adobe house and need more mud."

Hanson laughs and brushes his prodigious mustache—waxed and lifted at the ends, as if a bushy letter "w" rides his upper lip. His balding head is less impressive. The mustache clearly intends to draw attention from the carefully staged remnants of hair combed across the top of the man's head.

Hanson's smile is another matter. His lower lip peeks out beneath his handlebar, curved in a perpetual grin, as if the world amuses him. "Coffee for you as well?" he asks.

"I would be grateful for a glass of water," August says. "One cup of Texas coffee, and I'll be up until Tuesday."

"Ain't it so?" Hanson asks. He hurries off and returns with a mug of coffee and a Mason jar full of water. "What brings you gentlemen out this fine Easter?"

"Wasn't sure you'd be open, given the holiday," Ackerman says.

"Sunday's the only day some folks can buy their provisions," Hanson says, his eyes on August. "The mills are closed on Sunday, so I'm open, Easter or not. No liquor, though."

"Just water," August says and takes a sip.

Hanson looks over August's shoulder at the sound of the door. His expression changes. His gaze turns into a squint. He sighs and places his hands on the counter, palms down.

August steps to the side and looks back.

The man in the doorway casts a huge shadow, blocking out the Texas sun. He removes his hat, which is bigger than August Simms's chest, revealing hair clipped close to the skull. He steps inside the shop and runs a finger over his thick black mustache. Then, he sets his hat down and puts his hands on the counter. Hanson slides his own hands back, away from the man and his hat.

August stares at the largest forearms he's ever seen. Muscles like knotted rope. Popping veins. The man wears jeans and a denim jacket—a *Texas tuxedo*. By all appearances, a cowboy. When he speaks, the man leans forward so his voice can be heard. "Flour, sugar, and bacon," he says. The words are soft gravel.

August heads for the tables. Ackerman is there first, pulling out a chair for him.

Nute watches the big man at the counter. His upper lip curls back, and he scratches his stubbled chin.

August clears his throat. "I enjoyed talking to you about the flying machine, Mr. Rivers."

"Nute."

"Nute, then. Call me August." He wants to continue talking, but Nute's eyes are on the cowboy. Hanson returns with bags of flour and sugar, along with a wrapped parcel of bacon. Hanson places a ledger book up on the counter, saying "Make your mark." The big man takes the offered fountain pen and stares at the book. "Right here," Hanson adds, pointing to a spot in the ledger. The cowboy leans forward and scratches the pen on the page.

"Credit," Nute says, snorting.

Ackerman smiles and takes a sip of coffee. "I have an account here, too." He sets the cup down. The coffee is the same color as the cowboy's skin.

"There's credit, and then there's credit," Nute says.

August is still smiling. "How so?"

"Well," Ackerman says, lowering his voice. The word is extended, like wire pulled through a drawing die. August waits.

"Small town," Ackerman continues. "Hanson scrabbles to make ends meet. A little credit helps all the folks." He pauses. "Besides, Hanson won't let anyone get in too deep."

"If he did," Nute says, "they'd just run off. Happens all the time."

Ackerman nods in the big cowboy's direction. "His sister Abigail vouches for his account. She's got a house and a few animals. Collateral security." Another sip of coffee. "Bose Williams cowboys for a ranch west of here. When he comes back to town, he stays with Abigail."

August knows the names.

"Thinks he's a regular Bass Reeves," Nute says.

August knows that name, too. Black lawman in the Oklahoma territories. "Bose Williams is a big man."

"Big ol' boy," Nute says.

August frowns. "Let's talk flying machines." But the other two men are transfixed by the sight of Bose Williams scooping his provisions up in one hand as he dons his hat with the other. The cowboy glances at them, nods, and then steps outside.

"Big ol' boy," Nute repeats.

"That fellah hasn't been a boy in years," Ackerman says. Nute scowls.

August struggles to his feet. "Gentlemen, you have to excuse me for a moment. I'll be right back. When I return, I'll exchange coffee and sweets for your opinion of the much-heralded flying machine." He pats his shirt into place and heads outside. The shop window ensures a clear view of what's about to happen, but August is not concerned by that.

The cowboy loads his meager supplies into a buckboard. The swayback dobbin hitched to the front waits patiently in the hot sun. When the cowboy glances back, August asks, "Was your father Luther Williams?"

The cowboy faces him but doesn't answer.

"I knew a Luther Williams. He was a good man."

"My father been dead for fifteen years."

"I was here the summer he died," August says. "I knew him as an honest, hard-working man. I just wanted to say so."

August knows that people don't always know what to make of him. He adds, "I don't recall him being as big as you. He was more my size."

"Yep," the cowboy says. He climbs onto his buckboard, shaking the frame as he does. "Thank you for saying so," he says, voice soft as a whisper.

Back inside, August avoids the gazes of the two men at the table. Instead, he launches into an explanation of why he finds Nute Rivers to be such a compelling witness. "I have seen accounts claiming that the airships can go 100, 150, even 200 miles per hour. Those claims are absurd. No one had equipment staged to measure speeds. You, however," he says, turning to Nute, "were close enough to give a size estimate. You didn't say the craft was 100 or 200 feet long—and some accounts make those claims. Instead, you likened the size to something I can picture—a railroad car. We share a disdain for the news, Mr. Rivers. The long and short of it, sir, is that I find your account to be sincere."

Nute's gaze sharpens. The sun through the window lights his weathered face, shadowing the crags and turning his wispy hair translucent. "Thought I had some sweets coming."

August stands. "You do indeed. What's your preference, gentlemen? Licorice or peppermints?"

"A candy stick might help stir this mud," Ackerman says.

Nute shakes his head. "Hub wafers. Teeth can't stand any other."

"Done," August says. Hanson, still behind the counter, has been listening, and has the sugar wafers and a root beer stick ready by the time August reaches the counter. While August fishes in his pocket for a coin, a delivery boy puts a small stack of Sunday papers on the counter. Hanson nods at the boy and then takes August's coin.

"Enough left over for a paper?"

Hanson chuckles. "Sure. Let me get you change."

"Keep it." August tucks a paper under his arm and heads back to the table, candies in hand. "Hub wafers," he says, setting the candy in front of Nute.

The old man doesn't reach for the sweets. Instead, he stares at August, one eyebrow raised.

Ackerman takes his candy stick. "Thank you. Not big on sweets, myself, but this coffee needs a friend."

"So," August says as he eases himself into a chair. He puts the paper on the table. Ackerman picks it up. August is still smiling. "The airship sightings. What do you think is behind them?"

"Lot of theories out there," Ackerman says.

Nute shakes his head. "*I'm* wondering."

"What are your theories?"

"Not about the airship," Nute says. "I'm wondering how you knew that big boy earlier."

August considers his answer. After a long moment, he says, "I knew his father."

"His father died fifteen years ago." Nute pops a sugar wafer into his mouth. When he bites down, he winces. His teeth are not in good shape.

"1882," August says. "The summer the railroad came through."

"So, how did you know him? He was a murderer."

"I would prefer not to answer. Can we talk about the airship?"

Nute sits back, chewing his wafer. "Well then, *I* would prefer not to answer."

"Fair enough. I do appreciate the time you gave me. I found your account of the airship fascinating." August turns away, toward Ackerman. "What's in the news?"

Ackerman has the *Fort Worth Telegraph* open. He's frowning and the expression does not sit well on his face, which seems predisposed to smile. "More talk of war," he says.

"Oh, it's coming, by God." Nute slips another wafer into the left side of his mouth. He begins to chew, this time more carefully.

"I imagine so," Ackerman says.

The prospect is depressing. August slouches and rubs his eyes. He suspects his poor sleep is catching up with him. "It seems people feel compelled to beat the drum every twenty or thirty years."

"They'd be better off with a marching band," Ackerman says. He gives the newspaper a shake. "Say, here's another story about your mysterious aircraft." Reading on, his frown deepens. "This one is interesting."

"May I see it?" August asks. Ackerman folds the paper open and hands it over.

The Accounts of Two Gentlemen Regarding the Airship

Ladonia, Texas. April 17. Attorney E.M. Rowland informed this reporter of an airship sighting at 9:00 o'clock in the morning on Friday, April 16. Out for an early morning walk, the attorney spotted the craft to the southeast, moving very rapidly in a southwest direction. Though the sun was up, the airship boasted a bright searchlight, evidencing an electrical power source. The craft was cigar shaped, with huge wings and a tail like a mizzen sail.

A second witness, Bertrand Weldon, financial officer for the Ladonia National Bank, also saw the aforementioned craft. He was able to give a size estimate, which he stated as being 500 feet from stem to stern. He described the craft's progress as "swift," though he declined to approximate the actual speed. His description of the wings and the unusual tail structure varied little from Attorney Rowland's account, validating the testimony of both these stalwart members of the community.

"Interesting account," August says. "What do you make of it?"

Ackerman scratches his chin. "Sounds like two of our betters having fun at the expense of the little folk." He looks closely at August. "What do *you* think?"

August tries not to sound as tired as he feels. He needs another dose of his medicine and a good night's sleep. "I don't mind a good jest in its proper place, but the newspaper is no place for storytelling. Until I look these men in the face and ask them their version, I won't know if they're pranksters or men of substance, like Mister Rivers, here."

Nute nods proudly.

"Ladonia is a bit far for my poor wagon," Ackerman says. "A three-day ride each way."

"Perhaps I'll focus on witnesses a little closer to Rhome," August says.

"I'm glad," Ackerman says. "Bullet's glad, too."

August's mouth drops open. "Bullet? You named that horse of yours Bullet? He's as slow as a mud puddle."

Ackerman drains his coffee cup. "Yup. But he's ornery. If he could get a hoof through a trigger guard, I'm pretty sure he'd shoot me."

CHAPTER FIVE

Martins' Boarding house
Sunday, April 18, 1897

Ackerman's wagon drops August Simms in front of the boarding house at dusk. Clouds hang like gray pouches in the sky to the west, lit from below by the sun's last rays. A breeze carries the smell of rain. August walks the last few steps to the veranda and reaches for the damaged rail. He pauses and tries to catch his breath over the pain. He has been skipping doses of his medicine so as not to build tolerance. Today, he has pushed himself too hard, and he will pay. Pain management is a tricky business. Take too much, and the medicine becomes ineffective. Take too little and fall behind the pain. Once behind, catching up is difficult or impossible. He's behind now.

Bracing himself on the rail, he feels the wood give. He knows carpentry, and if he feels better, perhaps in another week, he'll tackle the job of repairing this rail. For now, he must climb carefully. If he falls, he'll ask for a blanket and sleep where he lies.

The thought makes him chuckle.

Nadine is waiting on the porch. "You missed dinner."

"Your Mister Ackerman and I—"

"He's not *my* Mister Ackerman," she says, a scornful look on her face.

"Pardon me," he says. His stomach flips. He wants to go to his room, take a dose of the liquid, and lie down. "If I might just—"

"I saved you a plate."

August smiles and shakes his head. "Thank you, but—"

"I saved you a plate," she repeats. "It's Easter Sunday. I fried a chicken, and I saved you a leg." She takes a breath, and when she continues, her voice is softer. "I know you don't eat much, but there's beans. Fried potato. A spoon or so of each. A slice of opera cake for dessert."

"I need to retrieve something from my bedroom." He looks to his right. "Could I impose on you? I would love to dine out here. Your evenings are quite peaceful."

"The clouds say rain."

"Rain would be welcome." Without another word, he goes inside.

Standing at the dresser in his room, he fumbles with the medicine bottle, dropping the cork. He tries to calm himself as he retrieves it from the floor. He is an old foozler, but it can't be helped. When his hands stop trembling, he takes a swig from the bottle, no longer interested in moderation. The taste is awful and he nearly gags. Then, still trying to calm himself, he corks the bottle. Setting it back in the drawer, he retrieves a peppermint.

Returning to the porch, he moves to the far side, around and to the left, nesting in one of the old wooden chairs. This is where he and his wife used to sit. The moon is nearly full, but the clouds have moved overhead, hiding the light. A gentle rain has begun to fall. The earthy scent of rainwater on dry soil makes him nearly weak with memories.

Across the field, a doe stands on long, spindly legs—still as a statue in the rain. The air is cool and a mist has formed, so his view of the deer is partly obscured. Far in the distance, a motte of trees stands like a dark sentinel watching over the horizon. The deer tilts its head as if regarding him. The sound of rain on the porch roof is settling, and he begins to relax until a lightning flash catches him by surprise. When his eyes adjust to the dark again, the deer is out of sight.

"Here you are," Nadine says, setting a small plate on the arm of a chair. "What will you drink?"

"A glass of water would be wonderful," he answers. There is far too much food on the plate, and he considers dumping it over the rail while she is off fetching his water. Instead, he takes a bite of the chicken. The skin is crisp and flavored with spice—paprika? The meat is dark and juicy.

"Here's your water," she says upon her return. "Don't expect me to wait on you every night."

"I did not expect it tonight. But I'm grateful. You are a wonderful cook."

She stands back, an odd expression on her face. "It's Easter."

He swallows his mouthful of food. "Will you join me?"

"I have work to do," she says, but then sits in the chair next to him.

August takes another bite of chicken. After he chews and swallows, he says, "Thank you."

"How long will you be staying, Mr. Simms?"

"Not long, I think." He searches the field for another glimpse of the deer. The young doe is gone.

"You said at breakfast that you're interested in the flying machine."

August nods, still chewing. One need not answer when one's mouth is full.

"Seems a foolish pursuit."

August must swallow, now. He takes a sip of water and then smiles. "I have been foolish for much of my life, so I can't argue. Old men are especially prone to tomfoolery."

"You're no fool." Her words sound like an accusation.

He sighs. "I spent some of my very early years teaching at a small college in Ohio. History was my specialty. The subject offers a number of intriguing mysteries, and I have become attached to such things."

"What kind of mysteries?" Nadine asks, settling back into her chair. A strand of hair has come loose from the bundle atop her head. It hangs down over her forehead. Her shoulders slump. She stares out over the field at the dark and the rain.

August shrugs. "The location of the Gardens of Babylon. Of Cleopatra's tomb."

"You were some sort of explorer, were you not? Did you try to solve those mysteries?"

"I did." August pauses to take a bite of potatoes, and then another sip of water. "When one does preliminary research, one begins with primary sources. Any ancient texts that survive. The theories of other researchers are interesting, but largely useless. One hopes to find correlations from primary sources—points of agreement that can serve as a basis for an educated guess. I will do much the same with the mystery of the airships."

She sits forward in her chair without facing him, her posture taut. "The same might apply to crimes that are committed. When there are conflicting accounts, one should put the testimonies side by side, looking for points of agreement. Then, form a theory and test it."

August cleans the leg and chews, not answering.

"And if three, even four sources say one thing, and the last source says another, then a lie has been told."

August shovels the last forkful of potato into his mouth.

"You said you knew my father," she says. "Please, go on chewing. I'll wait. It's a lovely night."

When he's had another sip of water, August says, "Yes, I knew your father. I was here in the boarding house the night he was killed." He shakes his head. "Sad affair. Do you remember much from that summer? You were young."

"Sixteen. I recall bits and pieces. Mostly, the funeral," Nadine says. She clears her throat. "I don't believe they ever caught the killer."

August stares at his plate. He could shove the slice of opera cake into his mouth, but she would wait him out. No use rushing a layered dessert. "Nor do I," he says.

She turns to him, her expression so intense that he finds himself instinctively leaning back. She pins him in place with her gaze. "The people in this town have a story they tell themselves about my father's death. I never believed it. I would appreciate you telling me what you remember."

August would rather discuss his quest for the airships. Instead, he will dig up the painful past. Senseless pain and cruelty can never be undone. The war convinced him of that sad truth. But he will give her what he can. "I remember that a man was arrested and held for weeks without a trial. Then he was released, and a second man was hung for the murder."

"Lynched," she corrected.

"Yes. Lynched."

"What was the name of the man they first arrested?"

"There's no reason—"

"What was his name please?"

August is too tired to resist. "Corn Norris."

"Corn?"

"Cornelius." August sips his water. The medicine has dried his throat. "You should know something else. Corn Norris died three years after he was released."

"How do you know that?" Nadine's voice spikes.

"I made it my business to know. He died in a derailment accident."

"He was a railroad man," she says.

"Yes. A railroad man."

The sound of a tap-*thump*, tap-*thump* announced William Chambers and his cane. "Hallo!" he says. "I've come to join in the conversation."

Nadine stands. There are only two chairs on this side of the porch, and William Chambers leans on his cane as if anticipating an open seat. When she speaks again, her tone is all business. "I have things to do before settling down for the evening. You gentlemen enjoy your talk."

August feels a twinge of regret. Despite the precarious nature of the conversation, he'd enjoyed Nadine's company.

Chambers drops into the chair and makes a noisy show of settling in. The groaning chair warns of impending disaster, but Chambers seems oblivious. "A beautiful evening," he says. "I have always been partial to rain."

"A soft rain is much to my liking," August says.

Chambers pats the strands of hair that cross the top of his head. "I wonder if I might continue this morning's conversation?"

"Certainly."

"You did not offer your opinion of the airship," Chambers says. "I wonder if you were reluctant to be candid in the presence of the women."

"Not at all." The thought tickles August, and he can't help but smile. "I don't have enough information to hazard a—"

"I've heard a rumor," Chambers says, a cryptic smile on his face. He leans closer—too close for August's comfort—and begins to whisper. "War with Spain is inevitable. You are a man of worldly experience, so you certainly recognize that fact."

"Actually, I'm hoping that sensible minds like the President's will intervene to prevent such a thing."

"Really?" Chambers draws back, surprised. "Surely, you support the efforts of freedom fighters in Cuba. They fight European tyrants, much as our forefathers fought the British."

The medicine is having its desired effect. August knows that he should go to bed now, before the wave he is riding crests and dissipates, but he is loath to move from the chair. The sifting sound of raindrops on grass soothes him. The long day's toll is paid. He will rest in the arms of the chair for just a few minutes.

Chambers is waiting for an answer. "You speak with passion for the plight of others," August says at last. "I find that admirable."

"True. I can't stomach the tragedies of others," Chambers agrees.

"The world in its present state must constantly vex you."

Chambers is silent for a moment. He squints and tugs at the bottom of his goatee. "I assume you feel a responsibility to your fellow man?"

August smiles. "I would prefer to fulfill such duties through channels other than war."

"Sometimes, war is necessary."

"Necessary? Exactly how?"

Chambers frowns. "If you are attacked, for example—"

"We have not been attacked."

"The good people of Cuba have been attacked. You've read of the reconcentration areas and the conditions therein?"

"Yes, I've read of them."

"Well then?"

"The matter is complex. Newspapers embrace sensation because it sells product. I wonder at the veracity of the New York papers. Money trails complicate the matter. Shipping companies don't like disruptions of trade, so they long for the forced resolution of conflict, as do sugar investors. I do not recognize the preferences of business entities to be *necessity*."

"But the Spaniards force the Cubans from their homes. They burn the crops and drive out livestock. And the camps themselves are a horror. How can you support that?"

"I do not, sir."

"It seems as if you apologize for the Spaniards." Chambers is agitated. His voice is becoming loud and he taps his cane, perhaps without realizing it.

August closes his eyes. He cannot discuss war without calling memories forth. Nestled here in a chair amid nature's soft, replenishing rain, those memories are an abomination.

"The President will negotiate with Spain," August says. "I am in favor of any steps that do not require young Americans to die on the field of battle. More, I do not think that lobbing cannonballs will have a beneficial effect for the people of Cuba. My opinions were forged on the battlefield, William. I saw much to dissuade me from an endorsement of any armed conflict short of self-defense."

The sound of his own name seems to calm William Chambers. He shifts in his chair, causing the wood to protest. The rain is stopping, but the damp air drapes the night with a blanket of calm.

"You said that you had a theory about the airships?" August asks.

"Yes," Chambers says. "As I said, war appears—at least to me—to be inevitable. I have heard that the airships are scouting coastal areas for potential invasion sites. Spain might be sending their airships to reconnoiter Texas."

August tries not to laugh. "Spain does not strike me as having the resources to build a fleet of airships. You may be right, though." He is tired now, in body and spirit, and wishes to end the conversation.

"Still, it's an interesting theory," Chambers says.

"The theory does not account for inland sightings, nor those in Iowa."

"What then? A prank?"

"That is a possibility as well."

"I don't understand you, sir."

August struggles to stand, grabbing the porch rail for support once he is upright. "Would it make you happy if I were to select one theory or another?" he asks.

Chambers doesn't answer, but August can make out his expression in the dark. A definitive answer is exactly what the man hopes for. "Well, then. I choose all of the above," August says.

"Pardon?"

"It would not surprise me if Spain sent a balloon to scout the coast. And a harmless prank perpetrated by well-meaning scamps, or even scoundrels, seems possible as well. Some witnesses may have even seen something miraculous. I spoke to Nute Rivers today, and his story was compelling. Others may be chiming in to join the fun and garner attention. I have not ruled out other possibilities—ones that challenge the imagination. *All* of those possibilities are in play."

Chambers gives his goatee another tug. "More than one answer is no answer at all."

August smiles. "But William, the real world is endlessly complex. With the ebb and flow of a thousand tides, *it's never just one thing.*"

CHAPTER SIX

Martins' Boarding House/Hanson's Mercantile
Monday, April 19, 1897

After breakfast, August returns to his room, only to find young Natalie at his dresser, studying his knickknacks and souvenirs. He clears his throat. She glances at him, and then returns her attention to the items in front of her.

August crosses the room, leaving the door open, and sits at the foot of the bed. He wonders at the young lady's nerve. She displays no evidence of discomfort at being caught going through his personal things. Instead, she grabs the brass compass and holds it up so the morning sun strikes the face. The glass is pitted and nearly opaque. She turns the compass back and forth. Seven inches in diameter, the instrument eclipses her small hand. "What is this?" she asks.

"A compass. The needle always points north. When you line the needle up with the N at the top, you can figure out every direction."

"I know how a compass works. But the glass is so dirty, I can't hardly see the needle."

"Yes, the compass suffered some damage. It comes from a submersible."

"What's a submersible?" she asks. Her brunette hair is pulled back tight with a headband. The rest spills down her back, unruly, as if it insists on revealing her true nature.

"A submersible is a craft that travels underwater."

Natalie's eyes grow wide. "Underwater? Men can travel underwater?"

"Yes. In this case, twelve men. And one woman."

"A woman!"

"Yes," August says. "My wife."

"How big was this submersible?" She has no trouble with the word, which August finds charming.

"The *Conger* was one hundred and fifty feet in length. She featured a hybrid drive with a gas motor for surface travel and an electric motor for underwater travel."

"Conger? That's a strange name."

"It's a type of *anguilliform* with a dark body and white spots along its length. The ship had a black body with tiny windows along the lateral lines. Electric lights inside. Underwater, it looked like a giant whitespotted conger eel."

"An eel." Natalie flinches and crinkles her nose. "I hate eels. When I was little, we went to Houston to visit Uncle Rhett. There were eels on the beach at Trinity Bay. They're disgusting."

"I can see why you would think so."

Natalie holds up the compass. "They could have spent a little more money for a better compass."

August chuckles. "It served its purpose well enough."

"Why do you keep it?"

August's smile runs away. "The compass is all that's left of the *Conger*. The ship and most of the crew are at the bottom of the Mediterranean Sea."

"Did your wife die, too?"

August sighs. "Yes, but not on board the submersible. She died here." He pats the bed.

"Here in this house?"

"Yes. Before you were born."

Natalie sets the compass down on the dresser. "I'm sorry. Did you love her very much?"

"Yes, I did."

Natalie touches a handful of fused metal nuggets. "What are these?"

"Pieces of metal that I took from the bottom of the ocean."

"Why?"

August laughs. "Because I have absolutely no idea what kind of metal they are. The pieces remind me that I don't know everything."

Next, she grabs the cannonball fragment. "What's this?"

"A souvenir from the Great War."

"What was so great about it?"

August's expression does not change. "Absolutely nothing," he says.

She sets the heavy fragment down and looks at him. "What is it exactly?"

"A piece of a cannonball."

Natalie runs her fingers over the rough edges. "I'll bet there's a story behind this."

"Yes," August agrees. "But it's not a fit tale for a young girl."

"I'm not a girl anymore," she says, giving him a tight-lipped smile that reminds August of Natalie's mother.

"Really?" August asks. "Because a lady would never go into a man's room and rifle through his things without permission." He says this in a soft voice that does not accuse. He is stating facts.

She blushes, bowing her head, though she doesn't break eye contact. "I'm sorry."

He decides she means it. "Apology accepted." When she starts to leave, he adds, "No need to go. You're already here, and I don't mind the questions. I enjoy your company."

She moves back to the dresser and points at his books. "Why these five books?" she asks. "Are they your favorites?"

"Yes, they are."

"I notice you don't have a Bible. Why is that?" August considers the question. While he thinks, Natalie continues. "I heard you quote scripture to Pastor Allen, so I know you've read it."

August taps his temple with a finger. "My copy of the Good Book is here."

"What's so special about *these* books, then?"

"Well," he says. "I will try to explain. Did you taste your mother's opera cake last night?"

Natalie squints at him. "Yes. What's that got to do with books?"

"Opera cake has five or six layers. Sponge cake. Buttercream frosting. Chocolate. Almonds." August closes his eyes. Nadine's dessert had been wonderful. He has a special affection for chocolate ganache. Eyes open again, he points at his books. "Each one of these has layers, like your mother's opera cake. Different flavors, each one delicate and delicious. They can be read and reread. Enjoyed over and over."

"Aristotle?" she asks, studying the spine of a book.

"A Greek philosopher," August says.

"I *know* who he is. I just can't believe you like reading this."

"I disagree with some of what he says, so revisiting the pages is like stepping into an argument."

"You like to argue?"

"I like to think. Real thinking happens when you consider both sides of a problem. Aristotle was a brilliant man. Arguing with him is a pleasure."

"How do you know who wins?"

"It's not about winning." August chuckles. "Except for the Sophists. For them, winning is everything."

Nadine arrives at the bedroom door. She knocks and then stops. "Natalie?"

August comes to the rescue. "I was showing your daughter my trinkets," he explains.

"My daughter has chores to do. Don't you, daughter?"

Natalie scowls.

"Mr. Ackerman has arrived," Nadine says. "He's waiting outside in that wagon of his."

August stands. Nadine wears a frown too, but it may not be directed at him, or even her daughter. She is a busy woman, and she has a day of work ahead of her. As Natalie slips down the hall, Nadine follows, shaking her head.

Her daughter, then.

Having learned his lesson the night before, August takes a healthy dose of medicine and recorks the bottle. After unwrapping a peppermint, he stares at the bottle's contents. He will need to visit the town's physician eventually. His supply is limited. After putting the bottle in the dresser drawer, he takes a brush to his white hair and goatee. He breathes into his palm and sniffs, worrying that the medicine makes his breath smell of whiskey.

Outside, Ackerman is waiting. Natalie crouches in the back of the wagon. "I'm going with you," she announces.

"I don't mind, but you need to ask your mother."

"I did," she says, crossing her arms.

"What about your chores?"

"She said they'd be waiting for me when I get back." Her voice is scornful.

"All right, then," August turns to Ackerman. "Shall we start at Hanson's? I'd like to read the papers."

"The train brings the papers by around ten," Ackerman tells him. "We should arrive just in time." He gives the reins a shake, and Bullet the horse raises his head. "Giddy up," Ackerman calls. Turning to August, he adds, "By the time you climb up, he'll be ready to move."

. . .

The papers arrive at Hanson's Mercantile before Bullet, so the latest news is waiting at the counter. Hanson greets them with a smile. Ackerman and Natalie go straight to the tables, staking out a place. August purchases one each of the three papers. He orders coffee for Ackerman, sarsaparilla for Natalie, and lemonade for himself. Then, papers tucked under his arm, he joins Ackerman and the others at the tables.

Nute Rivers wears the same wool suit he had on the day before. Wisps of hair jut in odd directions, as if he went directly from his pillow to the mercantile. He is nursing a shot of something amber-colored. He nods to August in an almost friendly manner, and August nods back.

The man sitting one table over is small, though his stature is enhanced by his proximity to Nute. He has a glass in front of him—empty—and the remains of a sandwich perched on crumpled paper. Ackerman introduces him as Joe Scully, railroad man.

Scully is cockeyed. August is unable to tell if he's looking at him or at Natalie. Perhaps both. He offers August a one-sided shrug of his shoulder. His half-smile and wink seem unsavory. "Who's this, then?" he asks.

"August Simms."

"And the girl?"

"I'm Natalie Martin," she says.

Scully frowns. "Your ma run the boarding house?"

"Yes."

Scully turns away.

Ackerman taps August on the elbow and shakes his head. August nods.

"Mr. Simms is interested in the flying machine," says Ackerman. His voice has lost its easy charm. He is all business now.

Scully turns back, his head tilted so that both eyes seem to fall on August. His half-smile is back. "Well, I seen it." He sits back in his chair, making it creak. He glances down at his empty glass. "I'll be glad to tell you my story, but storytelling is thirsty work." His gazes return to August and Natalie, his smile expectant.

August pulls himself up. His knees pop with the effort. "I'd be pleased to refill your glass in exchange for a story."

Scully nods. "A bargain for you." His expression changes again, as if his pinched, rodent-like eyes have located a piece of cheese. At the counter, Hanson obliges August with a glass of whiskey for Scully and helps carry everyone else's drinks. Natalie lifts her bottle of sarsaparilla and takes a huge swallow. Setting the bottle back on the table, she wipes her mouth with her forearm. Nute Rivers nods with approval.

Scully takes a sip of his whiskey, clears his throat, and says, "Understand, all of what I'm about to tell you is part of the record. Appeared in the paper, it did. They got things wrong, of course. Those boys have crossbucks for ears."

"What did they get wrong?" August asks.

"The news story said I saw the pilot scraping barnacles from the hull of the ship." Scully sits back and slaps his legs. "Like it were a damned boat! Like all the barnacles in the sky attached themselves to his hull, and he had to scrape them off with a chisel and hammer." His guffaw sounds like a shot. No one else laughs.

"Did you see a pilot?"

Scully is silent for a moment—face flushed. He takes another sip of whiskey. "Well, I surely did. He had a hammer and chisel, all right. But he was making some sort of repairs. Weren't no *barnacles.*"

"Where did you see this?"

"In a clearing, near Hawkins. There's an open space close to the water tank. The airship was on the ground there. Middle of the afternoon, and we were moving slow, so I got me a real good look."

"What did the pilot look like?"

"Tall man. Thin. Had a certain look to his eyes, like an inventor or a scientist."

August considers this. His glass of lemonade has gone untouched, so he takes a sip. Too much sugar. He shakes his head and returns his attention to Scully. "What made you think he was a scientist?"

Scully downs the last of his whiskey. "He had that faraway look."

August waits.

"You know. That faraway look, like his head's too full of thoughts and about to explode."

"Did he notice you?"

Scully scratches his head. "Well, now. I can't say he looked up. We passed by at about fifty feet, I suppose. Don't know that he paid me any attention."

"How big was his airship?"

"150 feet if it were an inch." Scully stares at his empty glass. "Answering questions leaves me parched, and this is probably a two-shot story."

August smiles. "No, you satisfied my curiosity. Thank you very much, Mister Scully."

"Every word is true." Scully turns to Ackerman. "Tell them my nickname."

Ackerman's expression sours just a little.

"Tell them!"

Ackerman clears his throat. "Joe is known to most everyone as *Truthful* Scully."

"An impressive moniker," August says.

Scully squints, tilting his head so that at least one of his eyes is directed at August. "Even the papers agree. One said, *Mr. Scully's.. . varsity . . . is on par with election results.*"

"Perhaps they mean *veracity*."

"That's it. That's the word." He gives the empty glass a mournful look. "I told what I seen to the boys in the clown car—"

"Pardon?"

Ackerman leans forward and taps August on the elbow, whispering, "The caboose."

"Ah." August chuckles. "What did your coworkers say?"

"They all believed me, of course. Everyone knows my word is solid as scripture."

Ackerman returns his attention to August's newspapers. Natalie seems intent on Scully's account, however. She has her elbows on the table, something August suspects her mother would never allow. "What did the airship look like?" she asks. "How high could it fly, do you think?"

Scully smiles wide, showing the gaps where teeth have gone missing. "Well, little lady, the ship looked like one of those Mexican cigars. Fat in the middle and thinner at the ends. A marvel. A miracle. The greatest invention of our age, or I'm not Joe E. *Truthful* Scully, freight conductor and man of his word." He leans closer as he speaks, and Natalie flinches. "I don't hold your ma against you. Just saying. You seem all right. You might not end up like her after all."

Ackerman has gone suddenly stiff. Scully glances at him once before backing away. Ackerman watches, a blank expression on his face. After a while, he hands August a newspaper, folded open to a story. "You should see this," he says, eyes still on Scully.

Mysterious Airship Crashes in Aurora

Aurora, Texas. April 18. Early in the morning, the residents of this small Wise County burgh were astounded by the appearance of the mystery airship that has garnered so much attention in the past week. The ship drifted over the sleepy town at a low altitude, headed due north. There, the ship's progress came to a tragic end on top of Judge Proctor's windmill. A terrific explosion followed, destroying the windmill and the Judge's vegetable garden.

The explosion scattered debris a hundred yards in each direction. The pilot, who did not survive the calamity, was disfigured beyond recognition. However, experts at the scene were able to determine that the pilot was not of this world. Some of the pilot's surviving correspondence appeared as unknown hieroglyphics, lending credence to the consensus of authorities.

The ship itself was damaged badly. It appeared to be made of aluminum, silver, and other unknown metals. Not enough of the wreck remained to speculate on motive power.

The funeral for the pilot will be held today at noon. Townspeople have pitched in to help the judge clear his yard and repair the windmill.

Judge Proctor. Another name from the past, reminding August of that summer so many years earlier. He had wondered if the old judge was still alive. Now, he would have to pay him a visit and inspect the site of the alleged crash. There was no avoiding it. They would talk about airships, but they would also talk about the hanged man. The thought turned his weak stomach, and the taste of lemonade bubbled in the back of his throat.

"Let me read that," Natalie says, taking the paper from August's hands.

"You'll want to ride out there, I suppose?" Ackerman says.

"Yes. Too late to attend the funeral."

"Two miles journey, some of it over fields. Old Bullet can do it, but it will take a bit."

August glances at Natalie. "I'd like to speak to Judge Proctor at length," he says. "We might be back too late. I don't think Nadine would appreciate us missing supper."

"She won't mind," Natalie says, her nose buried in the paper.

"Nevertheless, I think we'll go to Aurora tomorrow instead," August says. "I'd rather not be rushed." He turns away from the disappointment on Natalie's face. "Will that work for you, Ackerman?"

"Yes."

"Maybe I can go tomorrow," Natalie says, glaring down at her hands.

"We'll ask." August stands, fingers on the tabletop for support. "Mr. Scully?"

"Call me Truthful."

August nods. "Of course. I thank you for your time. Your story is remarkable."

Scully grins again. August thinks how wonderful it is that he's kept his own teeth in relatively fine condition. His one journey to the Indian subcontinent taught him the use of chew sticks, and the pharmacist in Baltimore made him batches of cinnamon and crushed eggshell to clean and polish. Scully clearly did not enjoy those same advantages.

August waits until the wagon is moving to press Ackerman for more information. "As regards Mister Scully's nickname?"

Ackerman's face is as sour as August has ever seen. "Truthful. They say he never stole a boxcar."

"Pardon?"

"He's a freight conductor who never stole a boxcar. That's what they say."

August frowns. "Are you jesting?"

Ackerman's expression sobers for just a moment. "No need for jokes. Sometimes, the world provides all the humor a man needs or can stand."

CHAPTER SEVEN

The Mill

Monday, April 19, 1897

Enough time remains in the day for August, Ackerman, and Natalie to visit the larger of the two mills. The newspapers listed the mill's foreman—Russell Walters—as another witness to the airship. August is also curious to see the new roller mill.

"Flouring feeds this whole town," Ackerman tells him. "Because we sit on the rail line, we can ship everywhere. Two mills' worth of business. Nobody comes to Rhome, but plenty of flour leaves." He turns to August. "You came here, of course. Not sure what's wrong with you."

August laughs, which hurts his chest. He groans and looks away.

Natalie sits in the wagon, directly behind August. "People used to come here. Not so much anymore." She thinks for a moment before continuing. "Ma says I must either take over the boarding house or marry someone who works at the mill. She says those are my only choices."

August closes his eyes and listens to the wheels of Ackerman's wagon rattle over the dirt road. Thumps when the wheel strikes a rut. The crack of pebbles. Bullet's steady complaints as he labors, hooves moving too slow for a steady rhythm.

"I know I've asked this before, but where would you like to travel if you had the chance?" August asks Natalie.

"Anywhere."

"How would you get there?"

"I'd wrap myself up in a flour sack and get myself shipped to Chicago by rail."

Natalie's answer is so cleverly preposterous that August bursts out laughing, hurting himself again. Ackerman glances at him with concern. "You all right, there?"

"I'm old," August says, which is true enough. August nods in Bullet's direction. "Your horse and I share some maladies, I suspect."

A lazy smile opens Ackerman's expression again. "Bullet was old when I got him. I wanted a wagon, and he came along with the deal. His original name was Lord something-or-other, which didn't suit either of us. Took me five minutes on the road to come up with a name that fits."

"You've had him as long as I've known you," Natalie says. "How long do horses live?"

Ackerman shrugs, his smile slipping away. "He'll stop pulling this wagon someday. Perhaps soon. When he does, we'll just walk these roads together and leave the wagon home. Won't be any slower than we are now."

As if on cue, Bullet stops and drops a load of apples onto the road. Ackerman sits still, reins in his hands.

"That's disgusting," Natalie complains.

"Actually, horses don't eat meat, so their poop is relatively clean," Ackerman says. "It's human poop you have to watch out for."

August can't help but laugh again, and this time, the pain causes him to double over.

Ackerman turns to stare, rubs his neck, and frowns. He starts to say something, then glances back at Natalie before closing his mouth tight.

"I'm all right," August promises. He looks to the horse. "Are more apples coming?"

"I don't know," Ackerman says. "I usually just wait. Pulling on the reins would be rude. Like banging on an outhouse door."

Bullet shakes his head and begins to pull. "Well, then," August says.

In the distance, the roller mill sits squat and flat, like a saltine box on dirt. It's the hottest part of the day. August smacks his lips and asks, "What's the owner like?"

Ackerman shakes his head. "Russell Walters is a hard man. I suppose you have to be hard to run a business—"

"My ma is hard. Hard on me." Natalie's voice carries a touch of pout.

Ackerman smiles. "His family came to Texas from Germany in the thirties. Settled in San Antonio. Poor family. His grandmother was a chili queen. Sold chili and tortillas in the plaza to make ends meet. His father died at Chickamauga. Fought with General Hood."

August squints. "You seem to know a lot about Mister Walters."

"He's a regular at Hanson's. As you've discovered, when you buy a man a drink, he'll tell you his stories to keep the whiskey coming."

Ackerman pulls the wagon into the yard and climbs down to take care of Bullet. A man comes out of the mill entrance dressed in tan overalls and work boots. His face, ruddy and covered in flour dust, appears pink from across the patch of dead grass. "Ackerman! Why are you and your *verdammt* wagon here in my yard?" As the man approaches, August can see his broad smile.

"Hello Walters," Ackerman says.

"I see that horse of yours is still upright. When he drops, remember. I have two hungry dogs at home." Walters rubs his hands together as if in anticipation.

"Bullet might outlive you, friend," Ackerman says. His voice is soft and friendly—a leaf drifting in a creek's current. August wonders at Ackerman's calm, given the discussion of Bullet's age just minutes earlier.

"Who is this?" Walters asks, looking straight at August.

"August Simms. Pleased to meet you." He steps forward, hand extended.

Walters offers a beefy hand in return. He is a large man with a square face. His belly pushes on the bib of his overalls, and the side buttons are unbuttoned to give himself a few extra inches. His grip is surprisingly soft—his palm as padded as his stomach. His gray eyes, by contrast, are sharp as vinegar. The man is measuring him.

"I've come to ask about the airship."

Walters snorts. "*Hör auf so Depp zu sein!* There is no airship."

August looks over at Ackerman, who shrugs.

"I was under the impression that you were a witness."

"*Ja*, I witnessed something. But it was no airship."

August tilts his head and waits. Walters hooks his thumbs into his overalls. "I pass the railroad tracks each night on my way home," he explains. "A freighter came chugging by, and there, by Gott, I saw the famous airship following. One light. Moving fast. Two men on the back platform of the caboose, holding the string."

"A kite?" August guesses.

"*Nein.* A balloon, shaped like a cigar. Big enough to carry a small lantern, for the balloon was lit. Idiots. If the toy crashed, it might have started a fire."

"The newspapers—"

"Sell newspapers. Fools buy them. I told the reporter what I saw. Didn't fit the story he wanted to tell, so he named me as a witness, and nothing more."

"Mystery solved," August says. He glances at the mill's entrance. "I understand that this is one of the new roller mills."

"*Ja.* First in the state."

"Might we take a look at the machines?"

Walters frowns. "Why?"

"Machinery interests me," August says. "New machines, more so than old."

Walters turns and strides for the entrance. August follows, though the foreman has not invited him to do so. Natalie, who held back at first, bounds ahead of him. Walters opens the door for Natalie and frowns. "Mind you now, don't touch anything if you wish to leave here with both your arms."

The interior is poorly lit. A row of six identical machines captures August's attention. Each is tall enough to reach his chest. The catch-bins on top are fed by pipes leading from the back side of the building. Belt-driven rollers grind the flour. Silt covers everything, and the sound is deafening. August stands very still, studying the machines. "The rollers are grooved steel," Walters shouts. "The other mill uses millstones. They make patent flour, but they can't match our gold medal quality." He frowns at August. "If I knew these machines were such a mighty wonder, I'd charge a dime for tours." He laughs at his own joke.

Men tend the machines and the feed pipes, sack and stack the flour on wooden pallets, and sweep the floors. There are a few small windows along the wall, but the sun is shining on the other side of the building, so the room is dark. The men look tired. When they glance his way, they take no special note.

A colored man with a broom passes between them. Walters grabs the man by the elbow and points. "Behind the machines, *Mist!*"

The man returns to the first machine, poking his broom into the two-foot space behind the roller mill, beneath the feed pipe.

Walters looks at August and shrugs. "*Neger.*"

"Thank you for the tour," August says. He can feel his face growing hot. Walters notices. He watches August with a raised eyebrow and the traces of a smile.

Back outside, August urges Natalie into the wagon. Walters follows them out, a grin on his face. "So sorry about your airship, though. *Das ist traurig, nein?*"

"*Ich werde überleben,*" August answers. Walters frowns.

Bullet seems anxious to leave the mill, so Ackerman has them underway in moments. In back, Natalie sneezes. "I think I have flour up my nose."

Down the road, Ackerman says, "You speak German. What did you tell him?"

"He seemed to think that his account of the airship saddened me. I told him I'd survive." In a lower voice, he adds, "A singularly unpleasant man."

Ackerman tugs on his ear.

"What are you thinking?" August asks.

"Well, I'll tell you." Then, he's silent for a long moment. "I'm thinking about the folks working in that mill. No sunshine. Breathing in flour ten hours a day, six days a week. Working like that is no kind of life."

"Ma says you don't work at all," Natalie tells them. "She says you're shiftless."

August is horrified, but Ackerman seems unperturbed. "You are mistaken, Miss Natalie. I am engaged in the hard work of human observation. I seldom allow myself a day off. The human race is a puzzle with ten thousand pieces. My work may never be finished."

August turns in his seat, glaring at Natalie. She looks away.

Ackerman continues as if Natalie hadn't interrupted. "Men were meant to work outside in the fresh air. Locked up in a mill? Not for me. I did that when I was younger. Won't do it again."

"If I were to begin an enterprise in manufacturing," August says, "I would install floor-to-ceiling windows. Men weren't meant to toil in the dark." He pauses. "However."

Ackerman smiles. "So, you don't agree with me?"

August very much likes this man. If he had more years left to him, they would become fast friends. "There's nothing wrong with what you said. Fresh air and light are necessary components of a good life." August glances to the side. A field of saw grass browns under the Texas sky. "But it's not easy to wrestle a living from the ground," he says. "Machines help. I've traveled much of the world and seen both sides of the argument. The tired men in that mill are struggling. But their struggle pales when compared to life without machines. I've seen men yoked to a plow, fighting rocks and hard ground. Their lives are spent before their third decade. No offense to Bullet, but some work is better left to horses."

Ackerman bites his lip as if chewing on a thought.

"My life's work centered around archaeology," August explains. "I studied artifacts, attempting to piece the past together. The story I eventually constructed is very different from the one written in most books. It's the story of past civilizations that wrestled with the same questions facing us."

"What question?" Natalie asks.

August keeps his gaze on Ackerman. Natalie was unkind to Ackerman, and unkindness is a sin of choice. "Civilizations are like children. They grow unevenly," August says. "Children are short, and then, suddenly, they shoot up so fast that their shins ache. Their feet are too large. Their ears too small for their faces." He pauses. He has time to make his point. Bullet is a storyteller's friend.

"Societies are much the same," he continues. "They evolve unevenly. When technology races ahead, it can be frightening. In the course of my research, I found past civilizations that made great advancements and then abandoned them. A perilous choice. They did not fare well."

He is suddenly aware of his pain. He has been hurting for a while but ignored it. Now, the pain takes center stage. The boarding house is not so far away. He will take his medicine and the symptoms will abate. "You have heard of the Luddites?" he continues.

"Yes," Ackerman says. "Textile workers, weren't they?"

"Yes. The Luddites demonstrated against mechanized looms in Britain. A man named Ned Ludd supposedly destroyed a textile machine in protest. I could find no evidence that the man actually existed, but his shadow, real or imagined, fell over the entire industry."

"Until Huddersfield."

August smiles. Ackerman is clearly well read. "Yes. The British government gunned down protesters and the movement disappeared. But that thread of protest against technology exists today, running alongside miraculous discoveries. Parallel lines that beg the question, *are we too clever for our own good?* I wonder."

"They say history repeats itself."

"If not a strict repetition, then certainly a persistent echo."

The boarding house is visible in the distance now. August can make out a figure standing on the porch. Nadine.

"Those ancient civilizations identified technology as the reason for their decline," August continues. "Though the desire to go back to a simpler past exists today, we live in an era where science is preeminent. This is the age of invention. Each new discovery is a revelation. But as human beings, we are only once removed from the caves.

"It's my belief that our civilization's failures lie with the philosophers and the poets. We do not have the proper signposts on the road to enlightenment." He sighs. The topic weighs on him. "Past civilizations turned their backs on technology and perished. We've embraced technology but we've failed to improve as human beings."

"What will happen to us?" Natalie asks.

"We're fixing to find out," Ackerman says.

Traveling on, Natalie wears a pensive look. "May I ask you a question, Mr. Simms?"

"Certainly." He maintains an even tone.

"Could the airship have come from the stars?"

"Anything is possible in God's universe, of course. But I think it's unlikely."

"I would like to study the stars," she announces.

"Why is that?" Ackerman asks, glancing back at Natalie.

"All this talk about airships," she says. "It's exciting. So much more exciting than Rhome, Texas. Do women ever become scientists?"

"Yes," August says. "My wife was gifted in the sciences."

"I suppose one must go to college," Natalie says. "That's not very likely."

"More likely than starships," August says.

When the wagon reaches the boarding house yard, Nadine strides toward them. Her face is a mask of fury. "What on earth did you mean, taking my daughter without my permission?"

August is baffled. Natalie had assured him that her mother approved of the trip.

"Get down off that wagon!" Nadine demands, and her daughter complies with haste.

"Now, Nadine—"

Nadine interrupts Ackerman's explanation.

"I don't want to hear it! There's no excuse!" She points at August. "You seem to think you are entitled to special privileges. One more bit of foolishness, and you're out! Do you understand me?"

"Perfectly," August says. "My apologies." He slides from his seat in the wagon and heads for the front steps, leaving Nadine and Ackerman to argue. Natalie brushes past him, nearly knocking him over on her way inside. The angry voices behind him recede. He wants to take his medicine and sleep. He will deal with any further repercussions in the morning.

At his dresser, he carefully uncorks the bottle of laudanum and swallows a dose. No need for a peppermint. He is going straight to bed. His gaze falls on one of his five treasured books—a bound volume of Shakespeare's plays. August recalls a line from one of the comedies. "To sleep, perchance to dream."

Given the choice, August decides that he would prefer the nepenthe of Odysseus.

CHAPTER EIGHT

Aurora, Texas

Tuesday, April 20, 1897

In the morning, August skips breakfast and walks outside. He pauses at the porch steps. A rock the size of a baseball sits on the top step. Behind him, he finds a gouge mark where the rock hit the front door. Wondering, he kicks the rock down onto the scrub grass and makes his way into the yard.

If Ackerman obliges him by arriving early, August will not have to speak to Nadine. Ackerman may have convinced her that Natalie talked her way onboard his wagon, but that won't alter her opinion of him. August has landed on her wrong side, which grieves him. He cherishes his memory of Nadine as a teen.

Nadine the adult approaches him from behind. "Mr. Simms."

He turns, hopeful. Her face is pinched. She squints into the sun as she talks. "Bill informs me that Natalie lied to gain passage on his wagon. I owe you an apology." One of her hands is clenched in a fist. Her apology has a cost.

"A misunderstanding. Nothing more."

"You did not join us for breakfast."

"I'm traveling to Aurora this morning. Ackerman—William— assures me that the journey will take much of the day. An early start seems important." August wants to take the sting out of the moment, so small talk is in order. "I don't know if you heard the news, but they say an airship blew up over Judge Proctor's farm. We're going to take a look at the crash site."

The furrows on her brow deepen.

"I know you don't give the reports much credence. I assure you—I nurture a healthy dose of skepticism. This is an opportunity to observe the site firsthand."

Nadine shakes her head. "I don't understand your interest. You came a long way to be here. Certainly not for idle curiosity."

Ackerman, Bullet, and the wagon appear in the distance. Right on time.

August gives Nadine his best smile. "I've had many adventures in my life. Why not one more? I want to see something miraculous, and though disappointment is the likely outcome, I wonder if the fabled airship might be what I'm looking for."

"I suppose this place holds additional meaning to you." She nods in the direction of her boarding house.

"Yes, it does."

Ackerman stops his wagon and looks down at Nadine. "Are we all friends again?" he asks.

Nadine shakes her head, trying to hide a smile. "Begone, both of you," she says. "I have work to do."

Ackerman's gaze follows her back to the house while August climbs into the wagon. "Aurora, then?" he asks.

Ackerman begins the arduous task of turning the wagon around. Bullet snorts and complains, but they are on the road in a few moments. The morning sky is clear and the sun is warm. "Bound to be hot today," Ackerman says. "Which brings up a question. Yesterday, you mentioned studying ancient cultures that abandoned their machines. I tried to think back to the reading I've done, and all I could come up with is Plato."

"Ackerman, you are a wonder. How did you get from hot weather to Plato?"

"Like this wagon, my mind wanders where it will."

August begins to recite from memory. "*An island, larger than Libya and Asia Minor combined, located just beyond the Pillars of Hercules.* According to Plato, the island sank under the weight of wicked and impious behavior."

"A predictable end," Ackerman says. "A cautionary tale for our great country. I believe the current call to arms will result in the quest for empire."

"Yes," August agrees. "We wring our hands over Spain's influence in Cuba, but our eyes are on the Philippines, half a world away."

"Did you find it, then? Atlantis?"

"Not per se," August says. "In my experience, many legends have a basis in fact, but the story of Atlantis was already a myth when Plato related it. Atlantis is a legend about a myth."

"You found *something*, then?"

"Underwater ruins. Some machinery that ought not be."

Ackerman drives on, chewing on his lip.

August leans against the seat back, relaxing. The morning air is sweet with the smell of privet bushes, like a memory of hay. The sun feels good on his back. His muscles are loose. The medicine is doing its work.

"What kind of machinery?"

August is startled. He'd dozed. "Pardon?"

"What kind of machinery?"

The underwater ruins. "Hard to tell. Some of it was encased in coral. But there were indications. Perhaps an internal combustion engine."

Ackerman sighs. "You've seen some things, haven't you?"

August pulls at his goatee. He enjoys this man's company. The beautiful spring morning feels good, and the dirt path stretches ahead like a road home. "I'd like to ask you something, if you don't mind."

Ackerman looks at him, squinting. "You're going to ask me about Nadine."

"She doesn't seem to like me."

"She doesn't *dislike* you. She's wary of folks in general. They've given her good reason to be wary. I wouldn't take it personally."

"Is there a story there?"

"Yes, there is, but I won't tell it."

"Fair enough," August says. "Instead, tell me how it is that you spend your days traveling here and there. Did a rich aunt pass on?"

"Uncle," Ackerman says. He chuckles at August's stricken expression. "I worked in a factory in Fort Worth for six years, or maybe it was sixty. Uncle Hermann left me a sum. The day the solicitor delivered the money, I quit and started walking. Went for days. Ate and slept where and when I could. By the time I hit Rhome, I had blisters, so I stopped. Bought this wagon with the intention of moving on, but it never happened."

"Must have been a sizeable sum."

"Not really. But if a man lives below his means, he can make a good life for himself." He clucks at Bullet. The horse ignores him. "What I told Natalie yesterday was true. The human species interests me, and I devote my time to their study. That's why I enjoy driving you around. You're an interesting specimen."

"I was just thinking that you had things to teach me as well."

Ackerman points to his right. A tiny shack and stable sit a hundred yards from the road. "That's my place," he says. "I own about two acres here. Just enough for a garden. A better man could coax something more out of the ground, I suppose. So far, I've raised some brown leaves and an onion the size of my thumbnail."

"Seems as if Bullet has the better accommodations." August notes. "You live alone?"

"Bullet and me."

"You might need a bigger place someday." He is thinking about his wife, Christy. She would have loved the little shack. He can hear her voice in his head. *So cozy! So romantic!* But she'd have set him to the task of adding on to the house almost immediately. "You might get married someday."

"Never happen."

"You could still fall in love."

"She loves someone else," Ackerman says.

They ride past a thicket along the road where a Bell's vireo sings its distinctive song. August can't spot the bird, for its drab coloring blends in well with the shrubbery, but the song—a warbled gripe—reminds him of William Chambers. He can hear the music in the call, so the bird's complaint doesn't bother him.

"My turn," Ackerman says. "I know you're not well. Exactly what ails you?"

"I have cancer," August says. "I think Rhome will be my last stop."

Ackerman exhales. "Well, I'm sorry to hear that."

August smiles. "Don't be. I'm eighty-six years old, and I've had more than my fair share." He turns to look at Ackerman. "My turn to ask, now. When you introduced me to Mister *Truthful* Scully at Hanson's, the topic of the boarding house seemed to anger him. You tapped my elbow, as if to say *don't ask.* I took your advice. But I'm curious now. What was that about?"

Ackerman gives him a rueful smile. "Not sure I like this game, but okay. Nadine won't rent a room to a railroad man. Everyone knows it, and the railroad men don't like it."

"Because of her father?"

Ackerman's eyes widen. "How much do you know about her father?"

"I was staying at the boarding house the night he died."

"Well, that explains some things," Ackerman says. "What you might not know is, the man who murdered Nadine's father was a railroad man."

"Corn Norris."

"So, you *do* know." Ackerman shakes his head. "I suppose you also know that another man was hung for the crime."

"Luther Williams. Father of Bose and Abigail Williams."

"I should have known. I watched you step outside Hanson's to speak to Bose, but I didn't know you well enough yet to ask more." He laughs, as if at a private joke. "My turn. What did you say to ol' Bose?"

"I told him I knew his daddy, and that I thought he was a good man."

Ackerman returns his attention to Bullet for a moment. The horse stops long enough to urinate in the road. "Going to have to find some water. Bullet needs to refill his pee bucket." When the horse moves again, Ackerman says, "I always wondered what happened to Corn after he skipped town."

"Died in a train derailing." Ackerman seems surprised, so August adds, "I kept track of him. His death saved me a difficult decision."

Ackerman starts to speak twice, coming up short both times. Finally, he licks his lips and says, "Guess you're nobody to run afoul of."

"I'm old and mostly harmless."

"Would you have taken things in hand yourself if he hadn't died?"

August forces a laugh and waves him off, saying, "It's not your turn to ask a question."

. . .

The astronomer's mother insists on serving the guests tea. August is anxious to move on to Proctor's farm but waits as the old woman delivers refreshments. The antique cups are decorated in gilt with a grape leaf design. The worn pattern shows its age. The astronomer's mother seems similarly fragile. August offers to pour, but she insists that she will perform the service. "I've had a bit of practice this week, what with so many newspapers wanting to talk to my Theo about the airship."

She pours a half cup for August, who holds up his hand. "Quite enough, thank you," he says. "Most generous of you."

"Did you read any of the news accounts?" Theodore Joseph Weems is a huge man, taking up most of a loveseat. Given the man's size, the loveseat appears to have been crafted specifically for its present use, rather than for the accommodation of two people.

Like the tea set, the furniture pattern is ornate but worn.

"I did."

"And what did you think of my account?"

"I'm afraid you weren't mentioned by name in the story we read," August says. "It was an early version. I'm certain that subsequent accounts were more thorough. The townspeople certainly know of your contribution."

"They insisted we stop by," Ackerman says. "I sure hope we're not a bother." He takes one sip of tea and sets down the cup.

"Not at all," Weems says. "And I'm not surprised they directed you my way. In matters like this, it helps to have an expert interpretation."

"What can you tell me about the explosion at Judge Proctor's farm?" August asks.

Weems clears his throat. When he begins to speak, he does so in a rapid-fire fashion that indicates a practiced delivery. "The airship passed through town early in the morning, heading north, traveling at a relatively slow pace—perhaps ten miles per hour. The ship seemed to be drifting, rather than following a definitive, predetermined course. When it struck the judge's windmill, it burst into a horrific ball of fire, consuming much of the apparatus in a matter of moments."

"You saw this?" August asks.

"No, no, but I did interview witnesses, including the judge himself. More importantly, I inspected the poor pilot's remains. I can say definitively that the creature was not of this planet."

"How so?"

Weems holds up a hand. "Though my credentials are in astronomy, I make it my business to keep up with advancements in all of the physical sciences, including physiology, anatomy, and the like. I assure you, even though the pilot's body was badly burned, I could ascertain the otherworldly aspects."

"Such as?" August asks.

Weems clears his throat, and August finds himself compelled to do the same. The room is small and stuffy. Looking up, August notes the ceiling is water damaged. A candle holder sits on a table against the far wall. Soot stains climb the wall behind it like a gray ghost. The hunched old woman does not seem capable of washing walls or ceiling, nor does her corpulent son.

"Simply put, the victim did not appear human. Though it shared certain aspects, such as a similar number of appendages, it was too small to be an adult human. Alas, the fire prevented any detailed analysis. Now, it's too late, of course. Summer is coming. Bodies must be buried quickly in Texas."

"When you say *a similar number of appendages,* what do you mean? Did it have additional arms or legs?"

"No, no. The usual two arms and two legs, though the arms were partially consumed by the fire."

Ackerman says, "The man who directed us your way said the pilot was from Mars."

Weems smiles. "As an astronomer, identifying the source of the airship is a contribution of some significance."

"Mars?" August repeats.

"Yes. In fact, I predicted the airship's arrival following my attempts to map the canals of Mars with my telescope. The first week of April is perhaps the best time of the year for direct observation."

"What kind of telescope do you have?" August asks.

"A refractor, of course. The lens was crafted in Europe, completely free of any chromatic aberration."

"Cost a pretty penny," Mrs. Weems says. "Those were better times."

Weems sighs. "My father was a professor at the University of Minnesota. I learned my trade there, under the tutelage of Professor Edwin Thompson. I took his course on practical astronomy. He even offered suggestions for the construction of future optical instruments."

"Then we came to Texas," Mrs. Weems says. "The University at Arlington offered my husband a position. We packed up, lock, stock, and barrel, and came to Texas like Davy Crockett." She shakes her head. "Halfway here, my husband—"

"Died," Weems finishes.

"His passing left us quite reduced," Mrs. Weems says, sniffing. "Theo's future died along with my husband. We simply did not have the resources necessary to pursue advancement."

"Astronomy is an expensive passion," Weems says.

"What was it in your observations that led you to identify Mars as the source of the airship?"

"As I said, I not only identified it, I *predicted* it. Did I not, Mother?" Mrs. Weems seems startled, and Weems rushes ahead. "I saw certain anomalies over the course of three nights. It appeared that one or more crafts were making their way across the solar system."

"How far away is Mars from our Earth?" August asks.

"Thirty million miles and more," Weems says.

"A long journey at ten miles an hour," Ackerman says.

August swallows his laugh, turning it into a cough. "You must excuse me," he says after regaining his self-control. "I am an old man and not from Texas. The change in climate has affected me more profoundly than I'd imagined. I do thank you so much for your hospitality, and for sharing your expertise."

Weems sinks back on the loveseat, putting August in mind of a sinking balloon. The man's lips are wet when he speaks again. "My account of events has been validated by its appearance in a number of respected newspapers."

"As you mentioned," August says. Ackerman stands.

"I received a degree in mathematics from the University of Minnesota," he continues. "May I ask, did you attend university, sir?"

"I was a professor of languages at Muskingum College in New Concord, Ohio," August answers. "But that was many, *many* years ago."

"Indeed. Our understanding of science has only recently evolved to its present apex. Many of the preconceptions of the past have proven false."

"An ongoing process, I'm sure," August says. He pivots, a motion that might have toppled him had he not had the back of his chair to steady himself. Facing Mrs. Weems, he bows. "You have been most generous with your time," he says. "And the tea was exquisite." Ackerman is already at the door, holding it open for his escape. "Mr. Weems," August says, bowing for a second time. "I am envious of your telescope, sir. I had the good fortune to look through the Trophy Telescope at the Crystal Palace Exhibition in London, more than four decades ago. That you possess an instrument which solved the problem of chromatic aberration is a wonder of modern optics."

Weems stands and offers a pudgy hand. "Perhaps you'll return some evening, then, and peer through my window to the universe."

"Perhaps I shall," August says. He grabs the man's hand with both of his and shakes. "I will look for you in the newspapers, sir."

The walk to the wagon takes an eternity.

Underway again, August says, "On our way here, you said you knew this man. What can you tell me about him?"

Ackerman closes his eyes as Bullet pulls the wagon along. "I met Weems years ago," he says. "He was in the Army Signal Corps. He collected weather information. A few years ago, the Department of Agriculture took that business over. After that, Weems left the army. I ran into him again when I needed some wheel work done on the wagon. By then, he was smithing. I don't think he lasted long. Smithing is a brutal trade. Not sure how he makes ends meet now. Doesn't look like he's starving, though."

"I take it that you did not agree with his speculations about Mars?"

Ackerman glances at August. "I hate to speak ill of a man."

"It's a sad thing," August says. "Presiding over a family's decline. I hope the attention in the newspapers is a balm for his wounds."

"Agreed," Ackerman says. "Now, it's my turn to ask a question."

"What do you mean?"

"You asked about Weems and I told you. It's my turn." He pauses, perhaps for effect. "What is a chromatic aberration?"

August feels his relief in his shoulders. He does not want a further discussion of Corn Norris. "Ah. Making a telescope lens is an imperfect art. Chromatic aberration is a sort of color smearing. A distortion. The sand used to make lens glass may have iron impurities, for example. Increasing the focal length of the lens diminishes the effect, but a skilled lens maker is of utmost importance."

Ackerman shakes his head. "I might have wanted to see the man's telescope," he says. "I've read about them. Never looked through one."

August can see a farmhouse in the distance. "I think that's the judge's farm," he says.

"Yes. Bullet's very good with directions." As they approach, it becomes clear that a devastating accident of some sort has taken place. The ground is scorched black, and bits of debris litter the ground. The wagon passes a swatch of material that still stinks of burned rubber. A two-foot length of metal pipe rests close by, blackened by fire. "Didn't the newspaper say that people pitched in to clean up the mess?"

"It doesn't appear so," August says. "This may be one of those rare occasions where the newspapers were mistaken."

Ackerman rewards him with an appreciative chuckle.

Closer to the house, August shifts in his seat. His stomach has begun to throb, and for once, the cancer is not to blame. The explosion, if that's what it was, seems to have blown out into the yard, away from the house.

As the wagon pulls closer, a man comes out on the steps. He is old, year-for-year as old as August. He holds himself erect with a hand on the porch rail. He is painfully thin, except for a tiny pot-belly. His hair is nearly as white as August's own. "May I help you gentlemen?" He pauses, squinting. His shoulders slump. "August Simms? Is that you?"

"Yes, Judge. It's me."

"Ah," the old man says. "I'd counted you dead."

CHAPTER NINE

Aurora, Texas

Tuesday, April 20, 1897

"The newspaper said you had a windmill," August says. Ackerman, August, and the judge stand around a stone well, a pit, and some burned timber.

"Stringers don't get things right," Judge Proctor says. "'It was a windlass. Eighteen feet tall. I used it to haul up sump water. Built it myself. Took two days to put a roof over it. Gone now." He is hunched over without a cane to brace himself. "Explosion blew thisaway—away from the house. Else I'd be spending my nights in a tent." He shakes his head. "Weren't much of a sound. More of a pop than a blast. I've heard dynamite blow. Weren't nothing like that."

"You saw the pilot?"

"After the fire died down."

"What did you think?"

The judge cocks his head. "I think that fire burned plenty hot. Made a cinder out of that poor fellah."

"We asked the same of Mr. Weems," August says. "He said the pilot was from Mars."

The judge coughs. "Well, I'm surprised Weems took his mama's titty out of his mouth long enough to answer you."

Ackerman turns away, shoulders shaking.

"If the pilot wasn't a Martian, it means somebody built an airship here on earth," August says.

"Couldn't say. I was over a stove, giving a pot of soup a third pass."

"What kind of soup?" The kind of question an old friend asks.

"Cock-a-leekie. Grew the leeks in the garden out back. Wrung the chicken's neck there, too. Good soup—gone, now. Like my windlass."

"You're a salty old bastard," August says. "I'm glad you're still alive. There aren't many of us left."

The judge nods. "A million stories will die with us." He meets August's gaze with an unwavering eye. "Some stories should go ahead and die."

"No," August says. "When those stories die, the world has to learn hard lessons all over again."

Judge Proctor turns away.

Ackerman gazes into the well. "How's the water, since the explosion?"

"I won't drink it lest it's boiled."

August peers down the mouth of the stone well. He can't see anything.

"What brings you back to this god-forsaken town?" the judge asks.

August flashes an embarrassed smile. "Came to see the airship," he says.

Judge Proctor sweeps an arm from left to right, as if introducing honored guests. "Well, here's your airship." He shakes his head, laughing to himself.

"I imagine you've spoken to a number of journalists?"

The judge starts back to the house, waving for August and Ackerman to follow him. "Oh, yes. Finest men in newsprint. Don't know the difference between a windmill and a windlass, or a man from Kansas from a Martian."

"The pilot?" Ackerman asks. "What makes you think he was from Kansas?"

The judge stops and looks back. "Because he looked like a cut of beef when the fire was done with him."

Inside the house, the judge fetches a bottle and a trio of glasses. He gestures at a small table, and Augusts sits. The farmhouse surprises him, not because it is cluttered, but because it's fastidious. The cupboard doors are all closed and the sink basin is spotless. The walls and couch upholstery are colored in yellows and browns, like a tintype come to life. Open windows let the smell of burned rubber in the room.

The judge pours two fingers of liquor into each glass, picks one of them up, and gestures at his guests. "Gentlemen?"

August and Ackerman each grab a glass.

The judge holds his glass aloft. "To the Martians. If it's my land they want, they're welcome to it." He downs the glass in a single motion.

August takes a sip and sets the glass down. Ackerman keeps his glass in hand.

Judge Proctor pours himself another whiskey and then moves to refill August's, but a hand over the glass stops him. "No, Judge," he says. "I'll gladly make do with one."

"Suit yourself," he says. Turning to Ackerman, he motions with the bottle.

"I'm fine right now," Ackerman says. "I have to drive us back to Rhome later. I'll need my wits for a journey of that distance."

"Two miles," Judge Proctor says, shaking his head. "Halfway to Oklahoma." Ackerman starts to speak again, but the judge waves him off. "No need to explain. I've seen your horse." He puts the bottle back on the table and turns to August. "So, is that what we're going to talk about? The airship?"

August nods.

"All right, then. What do you think of my little patch of scorched earth?"

"The canvas and rubber put me in mind of a gas balloon," August says.

The judge gazes without blinking.

"Carrying a heavy motor and framework aloft is work for more than just hot air. I would guess hydrogen was used, if only because the gas is flammable."

"Sensible. If up to me, that would be the last word," the judge says. "But I suspect the people of the town won't let it go."

"Are folks coming by to see the wreckage?"

"Yes, though all that's left is scraps. Weems and the smithy came by with a big wagon and hauled off some of the framework. Waste not, want not. Promise was, they'd be back to do some more cleanup, but Weems likely took his share of the scrap money in advance and considers the matter finished. I doubt the smithy even knew what was promised."

"What will you do now?" Ackerman asks.

Judge Proctor sighs and grabs his glass, emptying it before answering. "I'm too old to farm anyway," he says. "When I hung up the judge's robes, I told myself that I wanted to get back to the land. Grow something. I've been at this business since then. Damn near been the death of me."

"Farming is a hard life." August sits.

"Hard ain't the half of it. Like trying to milk a rock." He pours himself another glass of whiskey, smaller this time, and then corks the bottle. "I figure this airship foolishness is a signal for me to move on."

"Where will you go?" Ackerman asks.

"Far from this town."

August looks around the room. "Pity. You've got a nice place here. A home like this gives a man a sense of order."

"This ain't been *home* for years." Judge Proctor sips from his glass. His gaze hardens. "Seems like you've come to grips with what happened, though. Put it all to rights, did you?"

It's a pointed question, and August must answer. "Had to. I can't change the past, and I'm running out of future."

"Ha. No future for me here either." He stares out the window, as if seeing across the plain to the town proper. "Aurora could have been something. Railroad was supposed to come through here, did you know that? Went through Rhome instead. Now, there are jobs in Rhome, and nothing but dust in Aurora." He takes another sip. His hand has begun to shake. "I think folks are hoping this airship nonsense will draw visitors. Make a buck."

"How do they expect to do that?" Ackerman asks.

"Well, I'll tell you," the judge says. "I went to that pilot's funeral. He died on my land, so it seemed the right thing to do. One bright fellah couldn't wait for dirt to hit the casket before pitching his idea to me. He wants to organize regular parties to look for airships. Picnic lunches and beer included. He can't guarantee a sighting, of course, but he has that planned out. He wants to bring everyone out here at the end of the ride. Let them look at the burned ground. A grand finale. Offered me five cents a head. I told him he could come on my land any old hour, but if he woke me up, I'd pepper his party with my shotgun."

"Airship parties? Is that a real thing?" Ackerman asks.

"I saw something in the papers about it," August says. "They're already advertising in Fort Worth."

The judge slaps the table. "Jackanapes in *suits*. On *bicycles*. A wagon for the ladies." He glances at Ackerman. "Surprised you aren't in the business yourself, what with your wagon and all."

Ackerman chuckles. "A wagon full of women sounds like trouble."

"Ha." The judge raises his glass to his lips, but the glass is empty. He sets it down, uncorks the bottle, and pours a refill. He looks up at August and Ackerman, as if to ask if they'll join him. Both men decline. The judge recorks the bottle with some difficulty. "This whole business will be over in a week," he continues. "Edison wrote a piece about it in the papers, you know. Called it a stupid hoax."

"Thomas Edison?" Ackerman asks.

August is smiling, but there's an edge to his voice. "Mr. Edison aside, something did happen here, did it not? Your windlass did not destroy itself."

"And it came to nothing. Fire and wreckage—all there is to show. That's what we leave behind, you know. Fire and wreckage. Humanity is a plague that thinks itself divine. A pox on us all."

"A plague with the pox?" Ackerman asks. His glass is empty now.

"Eh?" The judge frowns. "What did you say?"

"The fellow who wants to run airship parties ought to visit Mr. Weems," Ackerman adds, trying to smile. "I'm sure he'd be amenable."

"Tell them all about the invasion from Mars?" The judge slaps the table again, leaning forward in his chair.

August puts a hand on the table. "Judge, I thank you for your hospitality."

"Leaving so soon?"

"Long trip back to Rhome. If we don't get to the boarding house in time, there'll be no dinner." He pushes his chair back.

Draining his whiskey, the judge slams the glass down and glares. "We ain't talked about it. We just going to pretend there's nothing to talk about?" He nods at Ackerman. "Does he know what happened?"

"No sir," Ackerman says. "I don't know much about anything." He turns to August. "Should I step outside for a moment?"

"No need," August says. "The judge and I will talk. But not today. I'll come back in the evening, when I can do more than wet my lips on this fine whiskey."

The judge tries to stand but falls back instead. "No, I believe we'll talk now."

"Judge." August's voice is smooth and low, like water slipping over a creek bottom. He pats the judge's sleeve. "I'll be back. We'll put the memories to bed, won't we? You and I?" He stands, using the tabletop for leverage. "It's damned hot outside. We've got a long ride ahead of us. I envy you, sir. You can lie down and let the day's heat settle."

"I can go lay down if I want to, or I can stay and finish this bottle. Whichever I choose is none of your damned business."

"Of course." August glances at Ackerman. "My friend here will have to help me to the wagon. It comes with age. Would you like him to help you to your room first?"

"What I'd like," Judge Proctor says, his voice drawn out, "is for you to stop patronizing me." His mouth hangs open and sweat runs over his lip. "Why did you come here? Digging up old memories, and all. Why?"

"The airship—"

"God damn that thing. Brought me all manner of bad luck. And it brought you."

"I'm heartily sorry for that."

The judge slumps down in his chair. "Well, then," he says, waving them off. "Get on with you. I'm tired." As August reaches the door, the judge clears his throat. "You come back, though. We still need to talk."

"We will. I promise." August closes the door behind him.

Outside, the heat is like a wall, stopping them in their tracks. Ackerman asks, "Do you need help getting in the wagon?"

"No."

"I thought not." Ackerman pauses to pet Bullet's neck and whisper in his ear, looking away while August struggles into his seat. The sun has baked the blackened ground. August can feel the heat through the soles of his boots. So hot in April! His lone sip of whiskey bubbles in the back of his throat. He longs for another dose of his medicine and a nap in a cool room. Silence, draped in shadows.

The wagon is moving—blessedly—and August prays for the journey to be over soon.

"Whose turn is it?" Ackerman asks.

"Whose turn for what?"

"To ask a question. I think it's mine. The judge was a little uneven there. You friends or not?"

"First things first. Judge Proctor is a good man, but I don't think he's much of a drinker."

"He put down a fair amount of whiskey in a quarter hour."

"The alcohol hit him like a sledgehammer."

"That it did. Will he be all right?"

August stares at the ground they're passing over. "Judge Proctor has a wounded heart. I'd hoped it had healed. It has not, nor is it likely to do so."

Ackerman is silent for a while. Bullet seems not to move, though the ground is still rolling beneath the wagon. "Does this have something to do with Luther Williams? With the lynching?"

"Yes," August says. "Let me tell you what happened."

By the time August finishes his dark tale, the wagon arrives at the boarding house. The hot day and painful retelling have drained him.

"Your story isn't so much of a surprise, given what I already knew."

August sits, hands between his knees, and tries to breathe. "I believe we'll stay close to home tomorrow," he says, listing the two stops he deems necessary. Ackerman agrees with a nod and waits as August climbs down from the wagon.

"Seems like the wrong folks are feeling guilty, though," Ackerman adds.

August doesn't answer. While Ackerman steers Bullet toward water, August musters a small wave and concentrates on reaching the front porch of the boarding house without falling.

CHAPTER TEN

Rhome, Texas

Wednesday, April 21, 1897

"Actually," the doctor said, "I've grown weary of treating lungers. It's a pleasure to attend to someone with your particular malady."

"Tuberculosis is a terrible disease," August agrees.

The doctor places the fluted end of what looks like an ear trumpet against August's chest. "So is cancer. Breathe deep."

"I am." August sits still, concentrating on his breathing.

"Cancer is a poison that spreads throughout the body. Some say it's contagious. I don't subscribe to that theory. I've often wondered if heredity is a factor. Tell me, did either of your parents die from the disease?"

"No. My father was killed in the Mexican War. My mother died from influenza a year later."

"Pity." For the first time, the doctor meets August's gaze. "Dying young, I mean." He is a slight man, perhaps in his forties. His clothing is black and vaguely formal, as expected of a proper physician. The first hints of gray appear at his temples, lending gravity to his appearance.

The doctor also smells of tobacco, and the odor turns August's stomach. "You smoke," he says, flinching as the physician leans in with his listening device.

"Medicinally," the doctor says. He leans back, again meeting August's gaze. "I suffer from nasal polyps. Tobacco is a successful form of treatment. And you? Do you smoke?"

"No." August has come for medicine, but the doctor has insisted on examining him first. The examination is proving to be a trial by fire, but he is willing to endure the man's poking and prodding in the name of securing the pain medication he requires.

"There was a time when tobacco was used to treat a number of ailments, from snakebite to constipation." The doctor turns away, scratching a note on a sheet of paper. "Many of these procedures eventually proved unhelpful. In some cases, even harmful. It was common, for example, to administer tobacco *per rectum* for certain hernias."

"Per rectum?"

"Yes. Basically, a tobacco smoke enema." He frowns at his notes. "Today, the medical sciences advance at an increasing pace. Much of what doctors know now is the result of studies conducted in just the last fifty years." He glances up. "I asked about smoking because the cancer has not entered your lungs. I thought perhaps smoking served as a deterrent to the cancer's advance in that one area." He returns to his paper, demonstrating concentration by the appearance of his tongue at the corner of his mouth.

August has come to the doctor's home, rather than asking him to ride out to the boarding house. "I am a guest there," he'd explained. "I don't wish to alarm anyone."

When August first arrived, the doctor apologized for the state of his quarters. Part laboratory and part living quarters, the single room is cluttered with a remarkable assortment of boxes, papers, bottles of various tinctures, and instruments of his trade—most notably, a fine brass microscope. "I usually visit my patients in their homes, where they presumably feel more comfortable." The doctor's explanation carries a hint of pique that August ignores.

Now, the doctor seems quite amiable. He sets his pen down, pushes the paper away from him, and turns his chair to face August with a sad smile. "My friend, it's time to discuss some hard truths."

"I'm dying."

"Your cancer has traveled the lymphatic system to other parts of the body. I find evidence of the poison everywhere. Except your lungs, oddly enough." He sighs. "I'm afraid there is nothing I can do. If the cancer were limited to one area, we might try surgery, but in your case? I suspect you are as much cancer as you are man."

"I understand."

"I wish there were something I could do. I've read of an experimental treatment that's had some success. A Dr. Coley, if I remember correctly, injected bacteria directly into the tumor. *Streptococci.* There are claims of efficacy. But I'm afraid that your disease is too far advanced."

"I know."

The doctor frowns. "Were you hoping for a second opinion?"

"No. I was hoping for additional pain medication."

"Ahh. I understand now. Perhaps you might have told me so at the outset."

"I did, actually. I suppose I did not speak loudly enough."

The doctor waves away his own irritation. "Well, I can certainly help in that regard." He stands and walks to a cabinet. "I've just three bottles and need to keep one of them here for personal use. Two bottles should last you until I can replenish my supplies."

"Most excellent," August says, relieved.

The doctor turns again. "You are lucky you did not call on my competitor. He prescribes a patent medicine of his own manufacture." His eyebrows knit with disdain. "After a chemical analysis, I determined just two ingredients—whiskey and gunpowder." He hands two bottles to August. "This, however, is the remedy that reputable physicians prescribe."

August takes the bottles from the doctor, careful not to drop them.

"You may not be aware, but even this will cease to be an effective pain deterrent as your disease progresses." August does not answer. "Nonetheless, I will order the necessary powders to compound additional supplies. I should be able to accommodate you before these are depleted."

"By all means, restore your supplies," August says. "But it's my sense that I may be reaching the end very soon."

"You've had medical training, then?"

"None, sir."

"Well, I am pleased to inform you that I disagree. You will almost certainly last a few more months. Perhaps as many as six. You're in excellent shape for a man your age, and the real pain hasn't yet begun. Don't be surprised if you're wrong. Remember, a little bit of knowledge is a dangerous thing."

"Words to live by," August says.

. . .

The second stop is the lumberyard. August hands over a small paper with some measurements listed. The foreman goes to work while August and Ackerman wait in the wagon. The sky is overcast without threatening rain, offering a pleasant respite from the heat.

"Where to tomorrow?" Ackerman asks.

"Tomorrow will be different. I plan to follow a lead from today's paper. If you would kindly deposit me at the train station by ten, I will travel to Fort Worth. There is someone there I hope to meet."

"For your cancer? Is someone advertising a treatment?" Ackerman asks.

"No. He's another airship witness. A judge. He supposedly examined one of the airships close up. He is, by all accounts, a respected member of the community." August watches as the lumber foreman cuts wooden dowels to the specified length.

"Is it all right if I drop you and the lumber off and head back to town? Or do you need help with this project of yours?"

"No, I'll be fine. You have plans?"

"No, no. But Bullet's been acting sluggish. I think he'd appreciate an evening at home."

"I'm wondering how you spot sluggishness in your horse."

Ackerman purses his lips. "He's right here, Simms. He heard everything you just said."

. . .

Back at the boarding house, August uses a hammer to tear the loose railing from the porch. He makes more noise than he'd hoped, and Natalie comes out to see the source of the ruckus. She stands still, hair tied back and hands folded in front of her like a doll. August ignores her.

"You still mad at me?" she asks.

"No use in that," he says, pulling another piece of wood loose. "A man could waste all of his energy waiting for an apology."

"I'm sorry."

"For what?" August sets the first dowel in place, not looking up at the girl.

"For lying to my mama."

Now, August stands upright. "And what you said about Mr. Ackerman?"

Natalie's face flushes red. "I didn't mean anything."

"Whenever you speak, you use words. Words mean something. If you don't mean anything, people will know it, because you won't be speaking."

"Are you saying I shouldn't speak?"

"I'm saying you should say what you mean and stand by what you say." He pauses to wipe sweat from his forehead. "Mr. Ackerman is a good man, and you insulted him."

"My mouth moves faster than my brain, I guess."

August motions her closer. "I need your help. Hold this dowel upright." He nods. "That's it. And I disagree, by the way. Your brain's as fast as anyone's. Faster than most. But you need to think before you say something. Words have consequences."

Natalie pouts, but she holds the dowel in place as he's asked.

"When will your mother be home?"

"She said she was going *out for the afternoon*. When she says that, she gets here right at suppertime. Once a week, like a clock. And supper's already cooked." She makes a face. "Stewed fruit and cornbread. It's the same every week. I *hate* stewed fruit."

"Well, I hate being hungry," August says. "So, stewed fruit sounds good." He ignores her sour expression and continues. "I once traveled to Greenland as part of a Danish mapping expedition. Our supply ship was delayed, and we had to winter without a proper amount of food. Toward the end, we ate a single meal every other day. Then half a meal. By the time the supplies arrived, we were near death."

"Greenland," Natalie scoffs. "Sounds like there should have been something to eat."

"Names don't always tell the story," August says. "Iceland is green as can be, and Greenland is locked in ice." He pauses. "For example, your name means *Christmas*."

"It does *not*."

"More specifically, it means the *birthday of our Lord*."

"Well, then. Every time you say my name, you should have to give me a present."

August laughs. "You are funny, young lady."

Instead of laughing with him, she turns away. Her sudden motion alerts him.

"What are you doing?"

Nadine's voice.

August stands back to admire his handiwork. "Almost done," he says. "Natalie helped."

"Who said you could do this?" Nadine's jaw juts out as she talks. Natalie starts up the stairs, leaving August to face the fury alone. "Well? Who gave you permission?"

"You did," August says.

Nadine's mouth twists in disbelief. "I did no such thing!"

"You said the porch was a common area, did you not? I am doing my share to keep order in the common area, as is our shared responsibility." He taps the front rail. "This was coming loose. Someone might have fallen. I'm an average carpenter at best, but I venture to say that this new rail will outlive us all."

Nadine sputters for a moment, clenching and unclenching her fist. "What am I to do with you, Mr. Simms?"

"A thank you would suffice." He is unable to keep irritation from his voice.

She scowls. "You might have asked me, rather than assuming—"

"I imagined it as something of a surprise," he says. He drops the hammer and begins to explain. "You and I have gotten off on the wrong foot, and I'm trying to make amends. I thought that a new porch rail would please you."

"It does," she says. Her voice is laced with frustration. "We are indeed off on the wrong foot, and neither of us seems able to get in step." She sets her jaw again and her voice flattens. "From now on, please, no surprises. This is my establishment. This is all I have. I must have my hand in all decisions. Is that clear?"

"Yes." August steps back. "I understand." He can feel himself shrivel, as if his shoulders are sinking into his back. Any energy he had is gone, and any desire for food along with it. The distance from the front step to his room seems like a journey of a thousand miles. "I find that I'm tired. I will enlist Mister MacGregor's help to clean up in the morning. Will that be acceptable?"

"I am serving supper in a few minutes."

August shakes his head. "I'm not very hungry." When he sees her expression, he thinks to lie. *I ate a large lunch.* He dismisses the thought out of hand. Instead, he decides that he must tell her about his cancer. It is his plan to die here, in her boarding house. She deserves to know. But he will not tell her now. He will choose a better time.

CHAPTER ELEVEN

Rhome, Texas
Thursday, April 22, 1897

In the morning, August steps out onto the deck to clean up the mess he made the day before. Ackerman is already present. The wood from the old railing sits in the back of his wagon and he is bent over the new rail, brushing fresh white paint onto August's handiwork.

"You've saved me a great deal of effort," August says. "This would have taken me hours. Tell me, does Nadine know you're painting?"

Ackerman chuckles. "She poked her head out once. Snorted and pawed the ground a little. Haven't seen her since." He returns to his brushwork. "I'll be done in fifteen minutes or so. We'll beat the train to the station."

But Bullet is slower than usual, and August is lucky to board the train in time. More, he's surprised to be joined by Ackerman as the train pulls out. "I had the livery boy take Bullet down the road," he explains. "I figure you could use a guide. I'm from Fort Worth. I think I mentioned that. Anyway, I'm curious to see how the city has changed." He scratches his chin and adds, "Besides, it would be smart to have someone along in case you take ill." His voice is casual in that drowsy morning way that Ackerman has.

"Kind of you." August realizes that his voice is clipped, but he can't help but chafe at the notion that he needs a chaperone. "Expensive, though."

"Today is a splurge day. I even sprang for a bucket of oats and some dried apples for that lazy horse of mine."

The ride into Fort Worth is a short one. They arrive before noon. The town's skyline is intriguing, with a handful of tall stone buildings mixed in with two-story businesses. August stares out the train window, mesmerized. A streetcar sits in front of the station without a horse to pull it. Wires are strung overhead, and August realizes that the car is electric. "I should like to ride that electric streetcar."

"Of course," Ackerman says. "Shall we go?"

August stands without wavering. Today is a good day. He feels energy coursing through his body. He pays the fare and boards the streetcar before August discovers that he has no idea where the car is headed. No matter. Destinations are not as important as the ride.

Later, when they gain their bearings, they change cars and arrive at the Tarrant County Courthouse, a striking multi-story edifice fashioned from pink granite. August is reminded of Italian architecture, though the building has been classicized with columns and a grand entrance that borders on the baroque. "Quite extravagant for Texas," he says. "The clock tower is tall."

Ackerman looks up, shielding his eyes. "Near two hundred feet."

Inside the courthouse, an imperial staircase flanks the rotunda with two separate flights of stairs. August bears left, which turns out to be the wrong direction. By the time they reach Judge Ford's office, there is a queue of visitors, and they are unable to meet the man until two in the afternoon.

Waiting reminds August of nights spent awake in bed. Finally seeing the judge is a relief.

Judge Ford seems a formidable man, tall and broad at the shoulders. His right eyelid has a pronounced droop such that his left eye appears preternaturally focused. His bearded mouth curves in a solemn frown, as befits his position. His hairline has receded, leaving a vast forehead lined with wrinkles and concern. When he speaks, he does so with a deep, rumbling voice that demands attention.

"What newspaper are you with, gentlemen?" he asks.

"I'm not with a newspaper," August says. "I read a brief account of your adventure with the airship and longed for more details."

"I am quite busy, as you can imagine." He leans forward, steepling his fingers.

"Yes, and I'm grateful for your time for that very reason."

The judge glances at the clock to his left, hanging on the wall. "That time runs short. What do you want to know?"

"The papers say you spoke to the pilot."

He sits back, his steepled fingers dropping into his lap. "Yes. I was fishing." He pauses, lowering his voice. "It surprises many that, despite my office, I enjoy several common pleasures. Fishing is one. I partook in that particular activity the Saturday before Easter past. As I was having no luck at my chosen spot, I moved downriver, where I encountered the famous airship that we've heard so much about, along with a crew of men."

"How many men?" August asks.

"Four. They were at their leisure, sitting on furs and smoking pipes. Quite friendly. They invited me to examine their ship, and I did so, careful to note details for any subsequent retelling of events."

"Would you share those details with me now? How large was the ship?"

"Less than forty feet in length. I am aware that other accounts describe larger ships, but men are prone to exaggeration."

August nods. "Yes, yes they are."

The judge returns the nod. "The ship was quite impressive. Three pairs of ribbed wings controlled by levers. The wings flap rapidly, allowing a direct vertical ascent, should the crew desire. I was allowed a glance inside. Living quarters with all of the conveniences, including bedding and a stove."

"Did you see the motor?"

"No, no. There were some secrets I was not privy to."

"Understandable," August says. "Did you engage in any conversation?"

"Of course. A judge is nothing if not a seeker of truth."

"What did they tell you? Where were they from?"

The downward arc of his mouth flattens, as if he were attempting a smile. "That is the most amazing part of the story. They come from a small nation, comprised of less than 300 square miles of territory located above the North Pole. After the dispersion of the Jews, the ten tribes of Israel attempted to cross the Bering Straits. En route, they were trapped on a floating iceberg, making their way to the shores of North Pole Land."

"North Pole Land?" August asks. "I've not heard of it."

"Few, if any, have."

"How is it that you understood their language?"

The judge's smile broadens. "They spoke perfect English. Are you familiar with the ill-fated voyage of the *Erebus* and the *Terror?*"

"Sir John Franklin's expedition, searching for a northwest passage."

"Indeed. The fate of the expedition has long been shrouded in mystery. Notes were discovered detailing Sir John's death. Several graves were located. The crew of the airship informed me that the remnants of Sir John's crew reached North Pole Land after their ships were crushed by ice. With no means for returning home, the crew stayed on. English was passed down to descendants as a second language."

"I thought it was cold in the Arctic," Ackerman says.

"Ah. The crew acknowledged that, in the absence of coal or wood, heat was a primary concern. What they had in abundance was *ice*. Ice is water, which is, in turn, comprised by hydrogen and oxygen. Oxygen burns, which allows them a heat source. Steam pipes keep the ground fertile and warm. As for hydrogen, that allows for excursions into the airy realms. It's quite natural that they have taken to the skies."

"Clearly, their scientific knowledge exceeds our own," August says. "I've read that the French use electrolysis to fill their military balloons with hydrogen, but that is a recent development." August sits back, suddenly lost in thought. The judge's office smells of oil soap and wood polish. A window behind the desk looks out over the streets of Fort Worth. Ornate metal holdbacks keep heavy drapes pulled open, but the room is full of dark wood, so the room seems dim.

Beneath the wall clock, a half-dozen picture frames display the judge's diplomas and awards. August glances at Ackerman. His friend is gazing at the same frames.

"The ship's crew intend to announce themselves to the press formally," the judge says. "They mentioned Nashville and the Centennial Exposition."

"What an event that will be," August says.

"Yes. Quite." The judge glances at the wall clock again. "Gentlemen, I hope I've satisfied your curiosity. I can entertain a question or so more, but my time is running short."

When August stands, he wavers and nearly falls. Ackerman steadies him with a hand on the shoulder.

"Thank you for your time," Ackerman says. August is silent.

Outside again, Ackerman asks what is next.

"The train station, I think."

"Are you feeling ill?"

"Run down, I suppose." He thinks for a moment. "My stomach is upset."

Ackerman points to a corner building a block away. "Whitsitt's drug store," he says. "We can get a Coca-Cola. Best thing for an upset stomach. Can you make it there?"

"I'll make it."

The drug store is a two-story brick building with striped awnings. The sign across the top of the awnings boasts *M. Whitsitt: Druggist and Chemist*. Inside, Ackerman buys two tall, rectangular-shaped bottles of dark-colored soda. They climb onto bar chairs and sip their drinks.

After a minute or two, Ackerman asks, "How is your stomach now?"

"I'm not sure," August says. "What's in this elixir?"

"I don't know," Ackerman says. "But I'm thinking about taking a few bottles home."

"Really?"

"No, I suppose not."

"You might as well. I thought today was a splurge day."

Ackerman shakes his head. "I'd like to get back, I think. Let's catch a streetcar and ride to the station."

August makes his way to the front door, past smoking products, bottles, packets of medicines, and chocolates. He feels better, owing to the stomach remedy. But the thought of the long ride home depresses him.

Conversation helps. While August gazes out the train window at the passing scenery, Ackerman asks about Judge Ford's story. "What was that about an expedition? Sir John?"

"In the 40s, an expedition was launched from England, traveling across the Canadian arctic to collect magnetic data and verify a northwest passage. The ships became icebound, and their crews were not heard from again. Their exact fate was never learned."

"Until now?"

August looks at Ackerman, noting the sly twitch at the corners of his mouth. "Judge Ford has an interesting imagination. Lost tribes of Israel and Sir John's lost expedition?" He muses for a moment, and then adds, "The judge has lost respect for his constituency."

"How so?"

August slumps in his seat. "His story was absurd to the extent that it bordered on insulting." He shakes his head slowly. "North Pole Land? I've explored the fringes of the arctic region. The story is preposterous. And the judge had nothing to gain by adding to the public record. Personal amusement is selfish motivation, but it's the only one I can imagine."

August sits still for a moment before continuing. The sun is setting, and the sky is melon orange. "There are people in positions of authority who put themselves high above the common person. They have nothing but disdain for their fellow human beings. They will lie, cheat, and believe themselves immune to consequence because their primary attribute is arrogance." He pauses. "Many of them become politicians. Others become civil servants."

"Astronomers?"

"Doctors as well," August says, thinking of the physician he'd seen in Rhome. "Arrogance unfettered is discouraging. I sometimes despair for my fellow man." He slides down further in his seat.

"Well, despair not," Ackerman says. "I'm here to balance the universe."

.   .   .

The sun is down when the train drops them in Rhome on its way to Folsom, New Mexico. Ackerman wanders off to fetch his horse and wagon. August waits at the station entrance, sitting on the stone steps.

The nickel-silver moon is more than half-full, and the night sky is clustered with stars—flickering lights that speckle the darkness. August locates *Capella*, one of the brightest stars in the open sky. With that star as a framework, he finds the outline of *Auriga*—the charioteer, which reminds him of Ackerman, who is taking a long time to fetch his own wooden chariot.

But when Ackerman returns, he is alone, carrying a lantern. His face is draped in shadows. He hands August the lantern. "I'm sorry. I won't be able to fetch you home. Bullet isn't doing well."

"What's wrong?"

"He's been acting funny for a while. Bought him oats and apples today, which he loves, but he didn't touch them. They told me he went to lie down in his stall and couldn't get back up. I tried to rouse him just now, and he gave it his best." Ackerman's voice breaks.

August sets the lantern on the step.

"I'm sorry you have to walk," Ackerman says. "I know you're tired. But I'm going to stay here tonight and keep old Bullet company. The vet says—"

"A vet already saw him?"

Ackerman nods. His eyes are glassy, shining in the light of the lantern. "The livery stable folks know my horse. They called the vet for me. Vet says colic. He's old. It's his time." Ackerman winces. "I'm going to keep him company. Maybe he'll feel better in the morning."

"Which way is the stable?"

Ackerman hooks a thumb over his shoulder. "Back that-a-way."

August grabs the lantern. "Let's go then."

"No. You won't get any sleep sitting in a barn all night."

"Were you planning on sleeping?" August asks.

"No. I'm going to stay with Bullet."

"Let's go then." August starts down the road. After a moment, Ackerman follows.

Their destination is a large white box-shaped building with *Livery Stable* painted on the front in faded letters that look gray in the moonlight. Underneath, in smaller letters, *Feed & Boarding. Buying & Selling.* A small, wiry man waits for them. Ackerman introduces him as Royce Jenkins, the owner of the stable. Jenkins leads them in through a door large enough for wagons to pass through.

Inside, Bullet lies half-on and half-off a pile of straw. August hangs the lantern on an overhead hook while Ackerman crouches near the horse and strokes his mane.

August sits, wedged into a stall corner for support. His pain medication has worn off and he is weary, both in body and spirit. He closes his eyes for a moment. The pungent stable smell is a strong concoction—equal parts hay, urine, manure, and leather. Underneath, the mellow fragrance of horsehair. The smell lulls him.

Ackerman whispers to Bullet. August watches the horse's chest heave. He's having trouble breathing.

At one point, Ackerman turns to glance back. "Are you okay?" he asks.

"I'm fine, Ackerman."

"You sure?"

"During the war, I went a four-month stretch sleeping on dirt and rocks. This is heaven."

Ackerman doesn't laugh. Instead, he strokes Bullet's neck. "Wish I had his blanket with me," Ackerman says. "It's an old wool blanket full of holes, but Bullet knows it's his. He ought to have his things with him. Ain't right, not having his things."

Later, August dozes. When he awakens, he has trouble moving his aching shoulders. The lantern casts a yellow pall over everything. Ackerman is sitting, legs outstretched, fingers tangled in Bullet's mane.

Bullet is pulling air in irregular gasps. Once or twice, the horse thrashes, but Ackerman is behind Bullet's back, away from his legs. When Bullet's chest finally stops heaving, Ackerman lays his head on the horse's neck.

August checks his pocket watch.

Just before midnight.

CHAPTER TWELVE

Rhome, Texas
Friday, April 23, 1897

The walk home takes forever. The lantern helps light the way, but each painful step reminds him how tired he is. He might have stayed with Ackerman in the barn until morning, but by then, the pain would have overwhelmed him, so he walks the road the old way—one absent, steady step in front of the other, a lantern in hand instead of a Spencer carbine over his shoulder. During the war, most officers rode on horseback. August marched with his men. He is marching now, crunching gravel to a beat that only he can hear.

When he reaches the boarding house, the door is locked. He sets the lantern down and knocks lightly on the door. No one answers. He sways in place, wondering what to do next. The porch chairs are around the side. He could sit until morning, though he longs for another dose of laudanum.

The door swings open. Nadine stands, one hand clutching the neck of her robe. "Mr. Simms. Do you know what time it is?"

"I'm sorry—"

"Are you drunk, sir?" Her words are terse and furious.

"Pardon?" August grips the porch rail, swaying.

"I don't say anything about your liquor, sir, as long as you keep it in your room. But banging on my door in the middle of the night is another matter entirely." She pauses long enough to shake her head. "Did you imagine that your peppermint candies were fooling anyone?"

"Ah," August says. He should have revealed his situation earlier. He feels foolish. "I apologize for the late hour, Nadine. But you are mistaken about the cause. Mr. Ackerman's horse took ill and died. I stayed with him at the stable until Bullet passed."

"Mr. Ackerman's horse?"

"Yes. Without a ride, my arrival was . . . delayed." August searches her face and sees what he imagines is compassion. He decides that the time is right for a full disclosure. "As regards the breath mints, I have not been entirely candid with you. I suppose vanity is to blame, but I can see that I've fooled no one. Whiskey is one of the key ingredients of laudanum. The doctor in town recently resupplied me. I take the medicine for pain. I am dying. Cancer is the culprit."

"Laudanum." Her voice has gone dull and flat.

August leans back against the porch post. "The taste is miserable," he says. "I assure you—I would not drink it for pleasure." He tries a small laugh. The lantern at his feet lights her face from below. He reaches down to grab the lantern's handle but stops when he notices the rock. This one has paper tied around it. He bends to pick it up, but Nadine beats him to it.

"What is it?" he asks.

"Just another prank," she says, her voice too casual to be anything but misdirection. She unties the string around the rock and removes the paper.

"What does it say?"

Nadine folds the paper without reading it and shoves it into the pocket of her robe. "It's a prank, Mr. Simms. Just like before."

August picks the lantern up and holds it near the door, spotting a second, larger hole in the wood. "Nadine? Are you in trouble?"

She tries to laugh. "Why would you ask that?"

"The holes in your front door have me wondering if someone is threatening you, or perhaps trying to frighten you?"

"Let's not change the subject, Mr. Simms." She tosses the rock over the porch rail and clutches the neck of her robe again. "Please don't repeat your late arrival."

"I won't. For what it is worth, my investigation of the airships is at an end. At any rate, Mr. Ackerman will not be able to provide any further transportation."

Her voice changes again—this time, softer, with genuine sorrow. "He loved that old horse."

"Yes. Bullet was very dear to him."

She bites her lip, as if considering a thought. "Mr. Simms. If you need a ride, you are welcome to my buckboard. I use it on Wednesdays to . . . run my errands. Every other day, it will be available to you in the event of an emergency. If you have additional need of the doctor. Or—"

"Most kind of you. The one place I intend to continue visiting is Hanson's, if only to read the news, but the mercantile is within walking distance." He pauses. "I do not intend to take to the bed until—"

"I'm sorry," she blurts. "I'm sorry you're ill."

"No, I'm sorry. I should have been frank with you. I suppose I was afraid you'd turn me away."

Nadine grimaces. "I'm not a monster—"

"Nor would I ever characterize you as such. I've asked you to let a stranger die in your home. You are not a monster. Perhaps a saint."

Her face reveals a series of expressions—surprise, amusement, skepticism—that she is unable to hide. "You are quite charming, aren't you?" she says at last. "But it's late."

August musters a laugh. "Yes. Please allow me to retire. I am sorry for waking you."

"Will you be having breakfast in the morning?"

"Yes," August says. "I think food would be advisable."

. . .

Breakfast consists of fried potatoes, sausages, and slices of homemade bread. August sits at the table between William Chambers and Thomas MacGregor. He scoops potato and a sausage on his plate, followed by a thick slice of brown bread. Satisfied that he has enough food, he looks up. MacGregor wears a sly smile. "Hello, stranger," he says.

"Yes, I've been on the road, haven't I?"

"Did you find your airship?" Chambers asks.

"Not a whole one," August says. "Pieces, perhaps." He takes a bite of the sausage, which is delicious. The fried potato is crisp on the outside, fluffy inside. He could not ask for a better meal. Four bites in, he is full. He tries the bread and it catches in his throat. He pours himself a glass of cider beer from the pitcher and washes the food down. Another bite of sausage? No, he cannot manage it.

"I dinnae ken how ye survive with no meat on your bones," MacGregor says. "I could put ye on a pole in the fields like a tattieboggle and scare the crows."

August snorts a laugh. "Shame on the crows, then."

"You found pieces of an airship?" Chambers asks.

"I can't know for sure. But I satisfied my curiosity on the matter."

"And what did ye decide?" MacGregor says.

August glances outside. If he's to do what he intends with the day, he will need to begin walking to Hanson's. "Why don't we spend the evening on the porch, and I'll tell you everything. I long to pass an evening in such a fashion."

"I would be pleased to join you," Chambers says.

August sees MacGregor's frown from the corner of his eye. "Absolutely, Mr. Chambers. Once the day cools, the porch here may well be the most comfortable place in Texas."

Nadine stands with her back to the table, shaking her head.

August rises from his chair. "I regret that I am unable to finish my breakfast." He turns to Chambers. "Will you help me avoid a tragic waste of food?" Chambers scoops the remains of August's breakfast onto his own plate while August returns to his room.

As he passes the stairs, he is surprised to see a colored woman on the steps. Her clothes are plain, but severe clothing does not hide her beauty. Her skin is a smooth, autumn brown—her eyes like burning leaves. She glances away as he passes, but he stops to engage her. "Hello. My name is August Simms. Do I know you?" He does. He is certain of it. "What's your name?"

"Abby."

Abigail Williams. Bose's sister.

"I'm not sure if you remember me. The last time I saw you, you were fourteen or fifteen years old."

She meets his gaze, her head tilted. "Perhaps I do." Her voice is measured and precise. The voice of a schoolteacher. Not a maid.

"My hair wasn't always this white."

Her expression relaxes. "Pumpernickel."

August Simms laughs. "Yes. Pumpernickel bread. You remember."

She looks as if she might smile, but then the spark is doused. He knows why. Too many memories and none of them happy. But she gives him a tiny nod, and it is enough.

Nadine walks into the hallway, glancing up at Abby and then back at August. "Mr. Simms? This is Abby Williams. She comes here on Fridays to help me keep this place clean. Too big a place—and too many men living here—to do it alone."

"I will try not to add to your chores," he tells Abby. He is laughing inside. Nadine never fails to speak her mind. She may think Natalie is too outspoken, but the child comes by her candor naturally.

In his bedroom, August takes a dose of laudanum and a peppermint, the latter being mere habit now that his secret is out.

Then, he returns to the hall where Abby and Nadine are whispering. They stop when they see him.

Nadine gives him a sharp glance. "Are you walking to Hanson's?"

"I'll be fine," August answers. And he is. The walk to the mercantile is bracing. The morning heat does not bother him. Rather, the sun feels like a warm hand across the back of his neck. He takes his time, step-by-step over the uneven ground. He concentrates on the taste of the air, the sound of the birds, and the smell of the saw grass.

Hanson's is busy. A half dozen men dressed in work clothes sit drinking whiskey. August doesn't like Hanson's lemonade, so he orders a Dr. Pepper. He pays for the bottled drink, along with a trio of newspapers, and heads for an open seat. "Mind if I join you?" he asks, standing before an empty chair.

The other man at the table purses his lips. He wears a somber expression. He is the only one of the men nursing a cup of coffee. The others are drinking whiskey. August knows one of them. Truthful Scully sits in front of an empty glass. At least one of his cocked eyes are on August.

Sitting next to the man drinking coffee, he says, "My name's August Simms." He offers a hand. "Yours?"

"Wilson." The man returns a brief handshake.

"Just Wilson?"

"I have some initials, but I don't use them."

August opens the first newspaper and says, "During the war, I tented with a man who went by his initials—BG. We spent the war coming up with outrageous and insulting possibilities. He never told us. Turns out his name was Bernard Gideon."

"How did you find out?"

"A letter in his jacket pocket. We found it when we buried him at Chaffin's Farm."

"Virginia?"

"Yes."

Wilson sips his coffee without further conversation, so August begins perusing news articles. The Fort Worth paper reprinted the open letter from Thomas Alva Edison on the subject of the airship sightings. Edison categorically denies the possibility of powered flight. Perhaps he imagines himself the only entrepreneur capable of inventing something wondrous.

"You ever find your airship?" The voice belongs to Truthful Scully, and the question initiates a round of laughter from the other men at the tables.

Wilson watches without comment.

August shakes the newspaper in his hands. "Mr. Thomas Edison assures me there are no airships."

"Well, I told you different," Scully says, one eye on August and the other on his audience. "If he was here now, I'd shove one of his electric lightbulbs up his—"

The loudest laughter comes from the oldest of the bunch. He is a thin, hunched man in bib overalls that are two sizes too large. Two fingers are missing on his left hand. Two fingers and a thumb missing on the right. He has a beard of sorts—a patchy mess of gray that extends unevenly beneath his chin. His mirth ends abruptly at the sound of the bell above the mercantile's entry door.

Bose Williams enters. He speaks so softly that August cannot hear him, though he recalls the last time he saw the cowboy in Hanson's. *Flour. Sugar. Bacon.*

"Just got darker in here," Truthful Scully says. His voice is loud enough to carry. "A whole lot darker. Is it clouding up out there? Maybe some rain on the way?"

More laughter. Bose stares straight ahead, waiting for his goods.

"A little too dark for me," Scully continues. "I take it back. If Mr. Edison was here now, I'd ask him to light up that bulb of his."

The older man with the scraggly beard slaps the table with his mangled hand.

August has half a bottle of Dr. Pepper left, but he heads for the front counter to order another. Bose glances to the side, and August offers him the same handshake he gave Wilson. Bose studies the hand and then takes it. The cowboy's own hand is crusted with callouses, but the grip is surprisingly gentle. Perhaps he is being careful with an old man's fingers. August says, "I knew your father."

"So you said." The voice is soft and does not carry.

"I knew you, too. When you were a boy."

"Yep. I thought on it after last week, and I think I remember you. You brought bread to the house after my father was lynched."

August closes his eyes. Murders and lynchings. After Luther Williams was lynched for the murder of David Martin—Nadine's father—August had delivered food to the Williams children. "I met your sister this morning. At the boarding house."

Bose winces.

"She grew up."

Bose turns his head and looks down at August.

"Seems like a nice person."

Bose turns back without another word.

"At any rate, it's a pleasure to meet you after all these years."

"Same," Bose says. Hanson has delivered the cowboy's parcels. He presents the ledger and Bose makes his mark. August returns to his seat, a second Dr. Pepper in hand. The other men at the table are silent, scowls on their faces.

As soon as the jingling bell announces Bose's exit, the older man asks, "What the hell was that?"

"It was a handshake," August says. "It's what men do when they're not fighting or fucking." The language catches them off guard. "I shook Mr. Wilson's hand, and I offer you the same thing, sir." He stands and extends his hand.

"No thanks. I know where that hand's been."

Truthful Scully laughs, and the others join him. Not Wilson, though.

"I can accept that," August says, withdrawing his hand. "Pleased to know the reason, though. I was worried that you were self-conscious about your missing digits."

"What did you just say?" The older man's voice betrays sudden anger.

"Let me guess," August says. "You're a brakeman for the railroad, or at least you were. And a damned good one, I'd say, given your age and the fact that so many fingers remain." The men at the tables are momentarily silent, mouths open. "I worked for the Florida, Atlantic, and Gulf Central before the war. Herd of cattle knocked the train off the rails. Three people died, and nearly everyone on board was injured." August taps his chest. "I broke a rib. Convinced me to enlist when the war started. I figured I'd be safer charging cannon than riding the rails."

"A quitting man, then," the brakeman says, his gaze narrowed. He might be ready to laugh, or he might be ready to throw a punch.

"No, a prudent one. I reached my dotage because I wasn't crazy enough for the railroad. Have you heard of the Devil's Gate?"

Truthful Scully snorts. "Everyone's heard of the Gate."

"I traveled the Loop in Georgetown just after it opened. One look at that bridge was enough to convince me to walk, not ride. It takes a special kind of courage to travel in the bow of a new technology." He glances at Wilson, who is listening, an odd expression on his face. "I imagine trains are safer now—"

"The hell they are," the old man with the scraggly beard says. "I have a cousin working outside Atlantic City. Express train hit a passenger train last year. Fifty people dead."

"Harrowing," August says.

"I was at the Crash at Crush," Scully says.

The old brakeman scowls. "That was for publicity. Ain't the same thing."

The previous fall, the owner of the Missouri-Kansas-Texas had staged an event with two empty locomotives rushing at each other at top speed. William George Crush had offered a cut rate to travel to witness the event, and more than 40,000 people showed up to view the carnage. Both locomotive boilers had exploded on impact, sending debris hundreds of feet in the air. Falling shards killed two people. "Folks died, publicity or not. Old Crush had the crowd stay back 200 yards, but he let the press stand closer." Scully chuckles. "No loss, if you ask me."

The others began chiming in with their stories. Every man in the room had a tale about an escape from death on the American rails. One told of a locomotive, behind schedule, that plowed through a terminal and dropped down into the street below. August had read of the accident, but it happened in Paris, France two years earlier. Perhaps the man borrowed the tale, having none of his own to share.

"That's all good," the old brakeman says finally, "but I have a question." He turned to face August. "What were you doing, shaking that boy's hand?"

August smiles. "I've known Bose Williams since he was a youngster. He's always been hardworking and doesn't say anything unless he has to. Fends for his family and doesn't ask for anything he can't buy. I'm guessing an old railroad man can appreciate that better than anyone. Am I wrong?"

The old man scratches his beard. "No, I guess not."

Having been given his cue, Truthful Scully agrees enthusiastically. "He's a good boy, as far as that goes," he says. "Not a troublemaker, like some."

As the conversation veers away from August, Wilson leans forward, both elbows on the table. "You're an interesting fellow," he says.

"Is that good or bad?"

"Neither one," Wilson says. He takes a sip of his coffee, winces, and sets the cup down. "Cold," he explains. "You can taste it better when it's cold."

"Is that good or bad?" August asks.

Wilson smiles for the first time. "Bad. So, you've been chasing the airships?"

"Ah!" August smiles. "You said *airships*. More than one."

"Seems likely," Wilson says. "That, or none at all. They say they caught some kids dragging burning tumbleweeds down in Waco. Trying to fool people."

"More like trying to set the state of Texas on fire," August says.

"What's your opinion on the matter, then? Many or none?"

August sits back. He has a bottle and a half of Dr. Pepper in front of him, and he will not drink them. His stomach is beginning to rebel. "I believe that some inventor or inventors constructed several ships. Gas balloons with motors to drive them. Wings for direction, perhaps."

"That would be remarkable. But why wouldn't they identify themselves?"

August meets the man's gaze. "I think one of the ships blew up in Aurora. Someone died. Death and explosions are no cause for celebration."

"I read that the Aurora explosion involved an airship from Mars."

August taps the newspaper at its side. "The story sold some papers, but that might be ending. The Dallas news has had enough. Today, they say—" He searches the paper for a particular quote. There—*A scientific lie is especially dreadful in its truthlessness.*"

"You don't think much of science, then?" Wilson wears a half-smile.

"A separate matter. Science asks questions. Scientists are questionable. The ones in the papers, at any rate." He pauses. "I believe that some men of great imagination and no small means have tried to take us skyward. As with the early trains we were just discussing, there are perils in the advancement of the mechanical and industrial arts. I wish them well and admire their courage."

Wilson stares at him for long moments, and then says, "As I said. You are an interesting man."

CHAPTER THIRTEEN

Boarding House Porch: Rhome, Texas
Friday, April 23, 1897
The weather takes a turn in mid-afternoon, so August begins the walk home. He'd hoped that Ackerman might stop by Hanson's, but the man was likely engaged in the disposal of poor Bullet. It was standard practice to saw the corpse of a horse into pieces that could be more easily handled. Sometimes, the horse was processed, its parts boiled until the fat could be isolated and used for fertilizer or glue. August knew of such a place off the south edge of Brooklyn on the East Coast. The plant handled as many as twenty thousand horses a year. Because the boiled bones were dropped into the Atlantic, the area was known as Dead Horse Bay.

Ackerman, though, would likely give Bullet a burial on his land. If so, August would borrow Nadine's buckboard and ride out to pay his respects.

As he walks, August's thoughts drift to his own funeral arrangements. He needs to plan ahead, so as not to inconvenience Nadine. He intends to compensate her mightily for the trouble. Indeed, she will receive the bulk of his remaining resources.

The moment he became certain of his cancer diagnosis, August began liquidating his assets. Some of the money went to friends. An endowment went to Muskingum, his alma mater. What remained was not a fortune. He'd financed most of his own travels, and after his wife's death, he lost interest in monetary matters. But what remained would provide a small gift to Ackerman, who had become his last best friend, with enough left over to provide Nadine with the means to repair the boarding house.

He sees the house in the distance and cannot help but think of all that transpired fifteen years earlier. That summer had been an emotional firestorm. Nadine's father had been murdered—a crime that resulted in the lynching of Luther Williams, father to Abigail and Bose. He'd heard once that death came in threes. The death of two men had been followed by the death of his beloved wife. Christy was laid to rest in the cemetery in Aurora. He hadn't visited her grave—yet. He would do so when he called on Judge Proctor. But the gravesite was not important. What remained of his wife on this earth would be here at the boarding house. They'd waited for the end here. They'd said their last goodbyes here.

August arrives just as rain begins to fall. Not a Texas downpour, but a soft rain that might last into the night. Almost by accident, he has arrived in time for supper. Nadine serves braised elk with hominy and corn tortillas. August takes his customary small portion. Chambers has a full plate, but there is plenty left on the serving platter. Natalie is not present. Perhaps the others are saving food for her.

"Where's Natalie this evening?" he asks.

Nadine's back stiffens. "Natalie will not be dining this evening." Her tone of voice convinces August to change the topic of discussion.

"So, MacGregor. I can think of nothing better than an evening on the veranda with friends. Will you still indulge me after we dine?" MacGregor nods.

"I will be there," William Chambers says.

"Wonderful." August sets his fork next to his plate. "Nadine? The food was excellent, as always."

Nadine does not answer.

Outside, the soft rain raises a mist. August nestles into his customary chair. His morning walk left a pleasant ache in his legs. The cancer pain has abated, for the moment. MacGregor sits to his left, where August's wife used to sit. There are just two chairs, so Chambers struggles to bring a third chair around to the others, fumbling with his cane. MacGregor watches, a sly smile on his face, until August taps his knee. MacGregor shrugs and goes to the man's aid. For a while, the two men wrestle with the chair as if in a three-legged race. Finally, Chambers lets MacGregor carry the chair while he follows.

Settled, August is surprised to see a deer no more than thirty yards away. Is it the same doe he spotted days before? He can't tell for sure. She looks the same, and she's out playing in the mist, just like before. No one speaks, so when she moves, she does so deliberately, regarding them with no sign of apprehension.

Then, Chambers speaks, and the doe bolts away. "Tell me," he says. "Did you ever locate a flying machine?"

"Machines. I believe there may be more than one."

"A fleet?" Chambers seems amused. "I'd heard that some scamps were caught pranking people—"

"Yes, there were pranks. I understand that some railroad men were involved in one such ruse." August searches the meadow for another glimpse of the doe, but the animal is gone. "I believe that in complex matters such as this, there's never just one explanation. I visited a crash site in Aurora. The debris and fire damage show evidence that some sort of genuine catastrophe occurred."

"Ye won't be speaking of Martians, I hope."

"No, MacGregor. The debris was man-made."

The three men are silent then, watching the sky darken. "This evening carries a hint of my Caledonia." MacGregor's voice is as misty as the grass.

"What is Caledonia?" Chambers asks. He squirms in his chair, trying to get comfortable.

"Scotland," August explains. "Caledonia is the old Latin name for the land north of the River Forth. Since then, Caledonia's been used as a romantic name for Scotland. There's poetry in the sound, fitting for the evening."

"Ah, yes." Chamber nods as if he knew the answer to his question.

MacGregor waves a hand at the mist. "In Caledonia, of course, the mist is thicker and mixed with a drizzle."

"Like this?" Chambers asks.

"No. Much, much thicker," MacGregor says, stroking his muttonchop sideburns. "Scottish mist sits right upon the edge of a downpour, never seeming to turn loose. This?"

"This is nice," August finishes. "Just enough of old Scotland to feel the touch of home."

"Aye," MacGregor agrees.

August turns to his right. "Where's home for you, William?"

"Oxford, Mississippi," Chambers answers. A soft Southern accent, which has made no previous appearance, creeps into his voice. "Moved north to Illinois before the war."

"North and South? Which side did ye serve in the war?"

Chambers shakes his head, causing his goatee to sway like a pendulum. "I fought for the cause, I'm proud to say. Turned out badly, of course. Yankees burned Oxford to the ground as punishment for giving refuge to General Forrest." He taps his cane. "That's how my knee came to this sorry state."

"General Forrest? Were you cavalry?" MacGregor's voice sounds incredulous.

"No, no. I was with the commissary. Supply wagon overturned, and this poor knee was never the same." He sniffs. "I don't regret the sacrifice. Others lost everything. When they burned Oxford, all they left standing was the college and a shop or two. The Yankees were animals."

MacGregor grins. "Well then, Chambers. We're brothers-in-arms. I fought with General Hood." He leans forward, talking past

August. "And how do ye feel about the end of our peculiar institution?"

"Well," Chambers says, his voice dropping to a lower register, "my family didn't own slaves. Father was a clerk. None of the men I served with owned slaves. But I would point out that *freedom*"— he dragged the word out for emphasis— "hasn't done the colored folk any good. Drunks and criminals, even here in Rhome. I fear that circumstances have done the colored race a great harm."

"You fought for the North, did ye not?" MacGregor asks August.

"You are playing the *bodach* this evening," August says, using the Gaelic term for a trickster.

MacGregor laughs. "I am a churlish old chancer, to be sure."

August turns to Chambers. "Our friend here knows that I fought for the Republic. In fact, I commanded colored troops at Chaffin's Farm."

"Oh." The man's face droops.

"Here's what I learned from my experiences, William. It was customary to have colored troops spearhead an assault. Perhaps they were regarded as expendable, but the men I commanded were *anxious* to fight. They wanted to prove that they were the equal of any white soldier, so they took chances. They charged battlements that would have turned others away."

"I would never argue the ferocity of the black race," Chambers says.

"I'm speaking about courage."

"Oh, they can be courageous," Chambers says. "I've known some who had no fear whatsoever."

August purses his lips and sits back. This is a conversation he would have liked to avoid. He doubts that William Chambers ever faced enemy fire. Perhaps his knee prevented service in that capacity. Still, the man's assumptions grate on him. August wants a quiet night, swapping stories in the rain, but MacGregor is stirring a pot, and Chambers is being Chambers.

"My experience may be different than yours, William. The men I commanded were afraid, but they did not let that fear dictate their actions. That, I think, is the essence of courage itself."

"I can agree with that," Chambers says.

"Excellent. With that as a criterion, I can properly express my admiration for the colored troops I commanded. They were the finest men I've ever known, bar none."

Silence.

August shifts in his chair, leaning toward MacGregor. "We charged the Confederate battlements and were turned back. There—I've understated the matter. I can't properly describe the carnage. For every casualty the men in butternut suffered, twenty of our men were killed or wounded. Three were later awarded the Congressional Medal of Honor for their actions. Every time the regimental colors hit the ground, another man picked them up, knowing that he would be the next target. No matter. Later, we regrouped and took the heights, through force of sheer will."

"It's a wonder ye survived."

"Yes, a wonder. I wonder about it often." August shakes his head at his own wordplay.

"I would guess by your mild nature that you were a good shepherd—"

"They were men, William. Not sheep." August closes his eyes and sighs. "Perhaps it is too much to ask that men regard each other as equals, despite the words of the founders."

"Surely, you don't advocate complete equality for the races. The founders only intended full citizenship for landowners—"

"Aye," MacGregor said. "And where exactly is your estate, my friend?"

Chambers gives him a rueful smile.

"My opinions in the matter are based on personal observation," August says. "That said, the men of color that served under my command were my equal in body, mind, and soul."

"But you are an educated man, sir. You've led a life full of adventure."

"A matter of luck. A heavenly blessing. I make no apologies, but I have no illusions. Given different circumstances, my lot would have been far different."

"Well," Chamber says. "I would not argue with you."

"You widnae win," MacGregor cackles.

Chambers glances past August to MacGregor. He frowns, sits back, and then leans forward again, his lower lip trembling. "Sir, you do not seem to like me. That grieves me because I have great admiration for you."

Though the sun has set, August can see MacGregor's face. His mouth drops open, but he does not speak.

August clears his throat. "The fact that there are three of us here on this porch guarantees that no matter the topic, there will be three different opinions expressed. That is the nature of men. Yet here we are, staying in this fine old house, sharing meals and stories. Three cantankerous old men." He turns to Chambers. "You're not quite so old, William. But you're getting there, eh?"

Chambers gives him a vigorous nod of the head.

"MacGregor, here, was an Indian fighter. I've traveled the world, yet I know precious little about the Indian wars. I could read the papers, I suppose, but it's better that old dogs like us learn new tricks from each other instead. I'm curious, William. What's *your* story?"

William Chambers smiles, surprised, and launches into his tale—a long history that begins with his father's bankruptcy and move north to work for his brother-in-law, a brooding, resentful shop owner who took a dislike to young William, whom he regarded as a shiftless dreamer. When the war began, William returned to Mississippi. His lack of physical stature relegated him to the supply train, where a freak accident damaged his knee.

After the war, he tried a series of occupations on for size, never finding a proper fit. He was a clerk, like his father, a teacher, a carpenter, and for one horrible summer, a farmer. "I killed more crops than the plagues of Egypt," he says.

MacGregor slaps his leg and laughs.

Finally, Chambers explains, the aforementioned uncle died. A widower with no children of his own, he left a small inheritance to his only heir. "I considered starting a business," Chambers explains, "but given my abysmal luck, I decided to retire and live within my means."

After a pause, he adds, "I never married. Never seriously considered it."

"Never fell in love?"

"Not enough to give up my freedom," Chambers says. "The benefits of marriage are plentiful, as God intended, but I prefer a simpler companionship. The one great love of my life was Oona." He pauses. "My dog."

"Eh? A good Gaelic lass's name," MacGregor says.

Chambers smiles. "She was an Irish Setter. Good gaming dog. Took her everywhere. Oona saw more of the states than most, be they creature or human." He grins. "She was a traveler, like you, August."

"What happened to her?" MacGregor asks.

Chambers is quiet for a moment. The sun is down now, and his face is masked in shadows. "She suffered from a congenital dislocation of the hip. Eventually, she could not walk properly, and as my life was regrettably nomadic, I was forced to put her down." His voice carries a hitch, and August waits without comment for him to continue.

"I had to shoot her," he says at last, and his voice breaks. "She trusted me implicitly. Facing her with a gun in my hand was the worst thing I ever—" A strangled noise comes from the back of his throat.

MacGregor fills the void with a story of his own. "At the Palo Duro Canyon, we were told to kill the ponies. Clatty business. The blackhearted bastard that gave the order widnae do it. Worse, the ponies kenned what was happening. They *screamed.* I shot one of them—only one. Poor thing pitched down and looked at me, thrashing. Shot it again. Then I walked away. We left the carcasses to rot. The bones are probably still there."

"God in Heaven," Chambers says. "How horrible for you."

"Aye." Now, there is a hitch in MacGregor's voice, too.

The air is thick with sorrow. Clouds, swollen with rain, block the stars. The wind sighs as August begins to shift in his seat, vaguely aware that his night pains will need to be addressed soon.

Across the field, the motte of trees stands like a dark, distant sentry. The outline is silhouetted against a lightened sky. The light grows brighter as August watches. He points across the field. Chambers leans forward in his chair, squinting. "Lightning?"

"Lightning comes in flashes," August says. "That is a steady light."

"What is it, then?"

The sound of footsteps causes them all to turn. "Gentlemen?" Pastor Allen's voice. "I've come to say goodbye."

August stares into the dark. The pastor's silhouette includes a valise. "You're leaving?" he asks.

"Yes," he answers. "Events demand it."

"Night is upon us," Chambers says. "Why are you leaving?"

"Events demand it," he repeats. "*Resist the devil, and he will flee from you.* John 4:7."

"Surely, the devil's not here in Texas," Chambers says. His voice is gentle, but the pastor is not amused.

"I will not spend another night in this house. You are welcome to remain, but *the prudent man sees danger and hides himself. The simple go on and suffer for it.* Proverbs 27:12." He turns and strides away, valise in hand. They listen to his steps as he crosses the veranda and climbs down the steps into the yard.

August stands with some difficulty and walks to the rail. Something has gone terribly wrong. "Pastor," he calls out. "I worry for you. It's a dark night."

"Yes," the pastor calls. "A dark night indeed."

CHAPTER FOURTEEN

Rhome and Aurora, Texas
Saturday, April 24, 1897

In the morning, August asks to borrow Nadine's buckboard. "My wife is buried in Aurora," he explains. "I would like to visit her grave. While I'm there, I will visit Judge Proctor."

"Of course," she says. Her face is lined like coarse linen. Her voice is hard.

"I intend to check on Mr. Ackerman as well."

Her voice softens. "Tell Bill I'm sorry about Bullet."

"I will." August pauses. He wants Nadine to have an opportunity to confide in him. Something terrible is happening. Pastor Allen's departure was an unpleasant surprise, and August has not seen Natalie since breakfast the morning before. But instead of speaking, she returns to her dishes. "The judge is fond of his whiskey and regards it a slight if I do not join him. Depending on the course of events, I may not return until morning."

"Fine," she says, speaking to the wall.

"Nadine—"

"No, Mr. Simms. There's nothing you can do."

August nods to himself and backs away.

MacGregor helps him with the buckboard. A sturdy quarter horse pulls the rig. "Billy is a fine fellow. Have ye driven before?"

"Yes, thank you."

"Aye. Good luck then." He steps back as August climbs into the buckboard seat.

"Plans for your day?" August asks as he takes the reins.

"Chambers wants to walk. He'll be *puckled* after a few steps but *mony a mickle makes a muckle.*"

August laughs. "Now, that's one I don't know. Mickle muckle?"

"Mony a mickle makes a muckle." MacGregor clears his throat and tries to approximate a Texas drawl. "Many small *thangs* add up to one big *thang.*"

August grins. "Get Mr. Chambers moving then and bless you."

The old Indian fighter gives him a terse grin. "Aye."

August's first stop is Hanson's. He wants a newspaper, and perhaps a Dr. Pepper. His plans change when he encounters the only patron in the mercantile seated at a table—bruised face cupped in his hands as if cradling the pieces of a broken vase. Bill Ackerman.

Newspapers and soft drink forgotten, August walks to the table and sits across from his friend. Both of Ackerman's eyes are blackened, and his lip is cracked and swollen. August asks, "What happened?"

Ackerman shakes his head—slowly—and mumbles through his damaged mouth. "Had a disagreement of sorts."

"How does the other fellow look?"

"Three," Ackerman says. "Three fellows. And they look fine." He draws a sharp breath and rubs his left side. "I think I cracked a rib."

"Who did this?" August asks.

Ackerman tries not to chuckle and winces for his trouble. "Railroad boys."

"Mr. Truthful Scully?" August guesses.

"My own fault," Ackerman says. "I was feeling sorry for myself and stopped in to drink some whiskey." He draws another labored breath. "That is something I'm no good at."

"Who started it?"

"That would be me," Ackerman says. "Talk got a little loose, and I've never been a fan of gossip. Decided to stop it."

"What did they say?"

Ackerman groans, as if from the memory and not the beating. "Prefer not to tell you."

August sits back, considering. After a while, he says, "A lot of mysteries around here."

"Well," Ackerman says, "today's mystery is how to get old Bullet home." His eyes begin to well up, and his voice breaks. "The livery offered me a little something for his carcass, but I couldn't see doing that. They—" He stops, shaking his head. "Royce and his boy cut him up for me, but there's nobody there today that can help me move him. I tried borrowing a wagon from a neighbor, but he needs his horse today. Bullet's starting to stink. Came down here to see if somebody would show up to help me. I don't know what else to do."

August stands. "Well then. Here I am."

Ackerman winces again. "I'm beat up and you're old. There's a grave to be finished, and Bullet's a load, even in pieces."

"I have Nadine's buckboard."

"It's heavy work."

"We'll work in shifts, then."

Ackerman looks up at August, sees that he's not joking, and struggles to his feet. "All right. Not a lot of other choices."

Ackerman carries a bucket of quicklime from the mercantile and places it in the buckboard. At the livery, Royce Jenkins helps them get Bullet's pieces loaded. Some are in parcel paper, open to the green-and-copper bottle flies. Bullet's head and neck are wrapped in a stable blanket. The hot Texas morning unleashes the stench, like rotten cabbage and feces, threatening to overwhelm them as they work.

On the road to Ackerman's house, August breathes through his mouth and tries not to speak. He's curious about Ackerman's fight, but his friend will talk if he wants the story told.

It appears that he does not.

Ackerman flinches with every bump in the road. August finally asks, "You need a doctor?"

"Probably," Ackerman says. "Bullet first."

Ackerman has two-thirds of a grave dug at the side of the house. Going deeper takes all morning and part of the afternoon, working in shifts. August wants to be of help, but the best he can manage are half-full shovels of clay that hardly justify his sweat. Every small rock stops him. Ackerman is in pain, stopping frequently to grab his side, but manages to finish the job.

August maneuvers the buckboard to the mouth of the grave, and together, they push the pieces into the hole. One haunch parcel comes undone, and Ackerman begins to weep. "I can't stand this," he says. "Don't let his head come unwrapped. I don't want to see it."

"Let me finish this," August says. He climbs into the buckboard and tries to nudge Bullet's head into the hole, but it's too heavy. He braces himself against the back of the seat and shoves the head into the grave with his feet. The blanket does not come loose. Climbing down, August feels dizzy. He sways and grips the buckboard for support. He can imagine himself passing out and tumbling into the open grave. When his head clears, he sprinkles quicklime over the pile of pieces and grabs the shovel. "Let's cover him up," he says.

Ackerman seems anxious to get a layer of dirt over his horse's remains but stops after just a shovelful. "A moment," he says. He limps away, returning in a few minutes with an old wool blanket. "This is his blanket. I'm going to bury it with him." He clutches the cloth to his chest.

August scratches his white goatee. "Are you sure you don't want to keep it?"

Ackerman thinks for a moment, his mouth open. He tries to speak and can't.

"Bullet will be plenty warm where he is, Bill. And the blanket might make a nice keepsake for you."

Ackerman sways in place. "I don't know what to do," he says at last.

August takes the blanket from him and folds it. "Put this back in the house. And give me that shovel."

Ackerman takes the folded blanket and returns to the house.

The dirt goes into the hole a great deal easier than it came out. With another half hour's work, they have a finished mound. "I'm going to plant some flowers here," Ackerman mumbles. "Something that will mark the spot. Something beautiful."

"I think old Bullet would like that," August says. He stands back. His clothes are soaked in sweat. The day has not gone as he'd planned. He still has things to do in Aurora. "Should we say a few words?"

Ackerman tries to speak and then shakes his head. "Can't," he manages. "Maybe later."

"Mind if I say something, then?" August asks.

"Please do."

August faces the mound, hands folded in front of him. "Dear Lord," he begins. His voice is thin and tired, but Ackerman doesn't seem to mind. "We humbly ask your blessing for Bullet the horse, who lived the sort of life any Christian man or woman might strive for. He was loyal, hard-working, and uncomplaining. Most of all, he was a good friend. As Bill here took care of him over the years, we ask that you watch over him now." He takes a deep breath. "The world you created, Lord, is not perfect. Otherwise, horses like Bullet would live longer lives, and men, perhaps, would live shorter ones."

Ackerman, head down, gives a slight nod.

"Perhaps your heaven is a more perfect place," August continues. "If so, may there be room for us sinners after the horses and dogs take residence in your loving embrace." He pauses to glance at Ackerman. "And Lord, please shine your blessings on my friend Bill Ackerman, who has a horse-sized hole in his heart today. Amen."

Ackerman turns away, his shoulders shaking. August puts a hand on his back for a moment and then turns to go.

"Thank you," Ackerman says through tears.

"I'll see you soon," August says.

Driving on to Aurora, August is heartsick. The day has gotten away from him, and his checklist of obligations seems to stretch ahead like the dry dirt road. He did not think to bring his medicine with him, and an overnight stay at Judge Proctor's now seems inevitable. He might save time by skipping a visit to the Aurora cemetery, but he won't allow himself to do so.

He parks the buckboard at the cemetery entrance. A fence runs along the perimeter and makes a nice spot to tie off the horse's reins. "Just a minute or two, Billy," he whispers. "When we get to the judge's farm, I'll see you watered and fed." A tree near the gate gives the horse a tiny patch of shade.

Farther on, a fence line thicket of hackberry trees offers food and shelter for a flock of bluebirds. Their low-pitched songs—two or three notes each—last no more than a second or two. They sound fussy, as if August's presence disturbs them.

He finds his wife's grave easily enough, though the headstone is small and simple. Writing takes up all the stone's face.

Christine Elizabeth Simms
February 5, 1819 – July 10, 1882
Beloved Wife
Step softly. A dream lies buried here.
~W. B. Yeats

The nearest tree is too young and sparse to offer any shade. Sweat rolls into his eyes, so August wipes his forehead with the back of his arm. His pants and shirt are dirty and he is exhausted. He stares at the headstone for a long time, nods, and turns to leave.

No.

Earlier, he'd spoken over the grave of a horse. He can muster a few words for his wife, can't he? He licks his lips. His throat feels tight and his tongue is swollen. He wishes he'd brought a canteen.

"The problem," he says finally, "is that I know you're not here. Are you somewhere? Maybe. But not here. This is where your body returned to the earth. Your spirit is somewhere else." He shakes his head. "I suppose I should say something on the off chance that you're listening."

Then he is silent again.

After a few minutes, he takes a deep breath. "I returned to Rhome, hoping for a miracle. Something new. I thought maybe I'd see a flying machine. That would be something, wouldn't it?"

He toes the ground. To his left, a dozen feet closer to the tree, a fresh grave. Is this where they buried the airship pilot?

"The miracle I wanted most, of course, was to feel your presence. I thought the boarding house was a likely place. You know I'm a skeptic when it comes to the hereafter. But I long for you, Christy. I've been—"

He breaks off and waits until the burning in his throat subsides. He dabs at the corners of his eyes with his fingers. "I thought that you might be waiting for me there," he whispers.

Nothing. Even the birds are silent. The only sound is the thrum of insects.

"Dear Lord," he begins for the second time this day. "Watch over my darling Christy. They say your love is limitless, Lord, and I hope that is so. But I doubt you could love her as much as I did." He pauses, and then adds, "As much as I do."

Tears roll down his cheeks as he returns to the buckboard. He feels her loss as keenly as the day she passed. His wound will never heal.

August unties Billy, climbs onto the seat, and urges the horse on without a glance back. He is ten long minutes away, and one more chore awaits him.

CHAPTER FIFTEEN

Aurora, Texas
Saturday, April 24, 1897
The judge sits on the porch of his farmhouse as the buckboard pulls up. Though August longs to sit and rest his bones, he sees to the horse first. The judge has a corral at the side of the house, home to an old burro named Peaches. August unhitches Billy and leads him to the trough. The water is murky, but Billy doesn't seem to mind.

"Old Peaches came around here when he got too old to be wild," the judge says. The burro is colored gray, with a white muzzle and ancient brown eyes. "I built this corral for him myself. Took me two days."

The uneven roof sags. "Looks like it's ready to fall down," August says.

"Well, you're pickier than Peaches. Doesn't look like your horse minds much, either."

"Anything to get out of the sun," August says.

Judge Proctor nods and waves him toward the porch.

"Is it always this hot in April?"

The judge shrugs. "Depends. Weather gets crankier every year. Tornados are the worst of it. One hit Denton County last year and killed near a hundred people. Sign of the end times, I suppose."

"End of our times," August says as they step inside the farmhouse. The front room is as clean as it was on his last visit. "Where's that bottle of yours, old man?"

"I'll fetch it," the judge says. "If I'd known you were coming by, I'd have cooked something for you. I already et. I've got some crackers if you're hungry."

"I haven't touched a molar breaker since the war. I'll just have whiskey, thanks." August settles into a padded wooden chair. "Pour me a glass, and we'll talk."

The judge fetches a bottle and two glasses. He pours far too much whiskey into one glass and hands it to August. Then he fills his own glass to the lip and sets it on a side table before easing into his upholstered chair. He takes a sip. "All right. Go on."

August smiles. "Where to begin?"

The judge sits back, his dark gaze locked on August. The judge is a hard little man—baked sinew, veins, and cracked skin like the bed of a dried creek. "After I stepped down from the bench, you came by to see me. Twice."

"Yes sir," August says. "As I recall, you ordered me off your land both times."

"I damn sure did. I wanted to forget what happened, and you kept coming around, sticking a finger in a fresh wound." He raises his glass and takes a second sip. "I do recall you saying you had a hand in the lynching."

"I said I had some guilt about the matter."

"I never did hear why."

August tilts his head. "You weren't in a listening mood. Would you like to hear the story now?"

The judge sets his glass down and sits back, one hand gripping each thigh. Steeling himself. "Go on, then."

August closes his eyes, as if the past resides on the inside of his eyelids, and in fact, that's where the past lies in wait for him most nights. "My wife was sick, and I went to town for the doctor. Wasted trip—he was off with another patient. On my way back, I saw the townspeople gathered. They were talking themselves into the lynching. Ugly scene. And I saw you, of course, trying to calm them."

Judge Proctor turns away, scowling.

"I'd seen mobs before. This one was like a pot at full boil. But I had a sick wife waiting, so I left. On my way back to the boarding house, I ran into Luther Williams. He did repairs and such for the Martins. Brought his kids along with him, sometimes. His daughter used to play with their daughter. That evening, Luther was alone. I stopped him and told him about the townspeople. I had some money in my pocket, meant for the doctor, and I gave it to him. Told him to get out of town for a while until things settled down. Told him *not* to go home—that I'd look in on his kids for him." August pauses to breathe.

"And that's it?"

August nods.

The judge shakes his head. "That's your burden? You gave him money and promised to look after his children?"

August takes a sip of whiskey before continuing. The sun will set soon. He will have to stay the night, as he'd expected. Hopefully, the liquor will dull the ache in his bones. "Yes, sir," he says.

"You're a damned fool."

August shakes his head. "Pitching money at a problem isn't the same as solving it. Besides, I knew perfectly well Luther would ignore me and go home to his kids. And that's where the mob found him. They hung him from a tree in his own yard. They spared the little girl, Abigail, but they made the boy watch."

"Going home was Luther's choice."

August snorts. "You ever have children?"

The judge shakes his head no.

"Christy and I couldn't have any. Tried, but we were never blessed. Given the same situation as Luther's, though, I'd go for my kids, and so would *you*."

The judge regards him in the dimming light. His hands are still braced on his thighs. At last, he says, "You had a sick wife to care for."

"Yes, I did. She died three days after the lynching."

"Well, I'm sorry to hear that. What ailed her?"

"Cancer."

The judge shakes his head. "Terrible way to go."

"So I'm told," August says.

"I suppose you might have done more for old Luther. But you didn't put a noose around his neck, did you?"

August sighs. "Neither did you."

The judge pries his hands from his thighs and settles into the chair. "I knew what those people were going to do. I could *smell* it. Sweat and whiskey and eggs gone bad. That kind of anger don't listen to reason." He sinks deeper into his chair. "But I tried to reason with them anyway. Told them to let due process take its course." He gulps from his glass of whiskey. "I knew they weren't listening, but I droned on like a parson. When they decided to move on Luther's home, I stepped aside and let them do their worst."

The judge coughs into his fist before continuing. "I spent my life tending the law. I told myself I'd done what I could, but I damned sure did not. And after that night, I wanted nothing to do with the law or the people the law was supposed to serve."

August clears his throat. He can feel the whiskey warming his insides. "It's not just the lynching."

The judge waves him off.

"Corn Norris," August says.

"That railroad son of a bitch."

"Corn sat in jail for *weeks*. No trial. When the townspeople asked when the circuit judge was coming, they got no answer." August pulls at his white goatee. "People have a right to be secure in their life and their liberty. When something bad happens, they expect that the law will address the situation, else what is government for? Instead, a railroad employee who murders a man sits in a cell, eating biscuits. Then, the railroad bosses arrive with a new witness who says he saw a colored man skulking around the boarding house. No surprise there—Luther was a handyman. All of a sudden, Corn Norris is out of his cell on a train with his benefactors, headed north."

"Those railroad sons of bitches were smooth. Came in on the afternoon train and left an hour later. No time to ask any questions."

August nods. "Left everybody feeling foolish." He leans forward, his gaze narrowed. "Foolish and *angry*. Meanwhile, the town had a new suspect. But what to do with him? Turn him over to the same law that just let them down? No. They took care of business themselves."

The judge looks confused. "You're not telling me those bastards were justified, are you?"

"No. I'm not. Some sins are unforgivable. If there's a hell, the men who lynched Luther Williams will go there. That includes the acting sheriff. I'm told he helped pull the rope." August takes another sip of whiskey before continuing. His head is going to swim soon, so he needs to make his point. "But right now, I'm talking about you. Tell me, who were the townspeople really mad at?"

"Well, that poor fellah they hung."

"No," August says. "I don't think so."

"The railroad?"

August laughs, but it's not a happy sound. "Not the railroad that guaranteed a prosperous Rhome when they bypassed Aurora. Oh, the town might secretly resent the high-handed way the railroad settled things, but they'd never say so."

"Who then?"

"They were mad at the *law*. David Martin, dead and buried with no accounting, and the law was just one more seat of power that could be bought. I'm guessing the railroad didn't want the publicity, so they slipped in and out, Corn Norris in hand, and left the townspeople looking like rubes.

"Along comes Judge Proctor," August continues. "Not the circuit judge, mind you, but the law just the same. You try to stop them because it's the right thing to do, even though you say you can *smell* their anger." August sits forward. "You're lucky they didn't hang you next to Luther Williams."

Judge Proctor sits back, frowning.

"You could have pressed the matter, of course," August says. "But they'd have turned on you."

"A braver man would have pressed them anyway." He looks away.

By now, the liquor has worked its magic. If August closes his eyes, he will doze. "I ran away in battle once. During the war. Skirmish outside of Richmond. Some rebels were lined up along a stone wall outside a farmhouse. We were supposed to take that house and set up a post. We could have charged them, but they'd have cut too many of us down. I had a wife at home, and the war was almost over. I saw no sense in dying for that little patch of Virginia dirt. So I turned, and we ran like rabbits. My sergeant was furious, but the men were relieved. That night, it clouded up and we came back under cover of darkness. Those rebel boys were long gone."

"You fought for the Yankees?"

"Yes, but that's not the point of my story."

"What is your point, exactly?" the judge asks.

One more sip, August thinks. The last sip, lest he make himself sick. "If you're going to risk your life, you ought to have a chance of succeeding. Otherwise, get the hell out of there. That mob would have skinned you alive rather than listen to you. You had *no* chance."

The light has begun to drain out of the sky. The judge clears his throat. "Now you sound like a lawyer trying to make his case."

"True," August says. "Here's my closing argument." He takes a deep breath, and when he continues, his voice is deeper, less conversational than it had been. "The townspeople of Rhome believe they did the right thing that night. They believed that murder ought to have consequences, and in my opinion, they were right. They believed that the legal system had failed them, and they were right. So, how did they respond? They circumvented the legal system and murdered an innocent man." He pauses to see if the judge has an answer. He does not.

"There's a difference between doing something and having it turn out wrong and doing something evil," August continues. "If I had that night to live over, I'd send Luther Williams back to the boarding house and then fetch his children myself. But I didn't want to lose even a moment with my dying wife. As it turned out, I spent her last three days weeping for a murdered handyman instead of focusing on her." He waits a moment before continuing, so his voice won't crack. "You, on the other hand, did what you could."

"Doesn't make it easier to swallow," Judge Proctor says.

"You feel some guilt? Fine. Those boys in town didn't, and somebody ought to. But you put yourself in exile for fifteen years, and that's not right either."

Outside, crickets sing the end of days. A faint glow at the edge of the horizon promises deeper colors to come—indigo, violet, and finally, black. The judge has an old glass kerosene lamp near the sink, but it sits unused. The momentary silence seems to fit the coming darkness.

"What were you doing in Rhome that night, anyway?" August asks.

"Wanted a bottle," the judge says. "Aurora was already dying, what with the railroad passing us by. Damned inconvenient." He snorts. "If I were a teetotaler, I'd still be on the bench."

"When my wife passed away," August says, "I buried her here in Aurora. There wasn't a graveyard in Rhome yet. I heard you'd resigned, and that grieved me. I knew you to be the one person who tried to stop the lynching, so I paid you a visit. I wanted to *reason* with you." August smiles at the irony. "Came back a second time a week later."

The judge snorts again. "I wanted to bury that night, and you wanted to dig it up."

August shrugs. "With my wife gone, I longed to put the pieces of the world right. I had Luther buried and saw to his children—"

"How long were you married?" The judge is beginning to slur his words.

"Forty years."

"Damn," the judge says. "You're a patient man." He taps his finger on his pursed lips. "I was married once. Her name was Arabella West. Big-boned woman. Couldn't cook a lick. I married her under a false name in case I didn't like the way things went."

August laughs—caught off guard. "What name did you use?"

The room is draped in shadows, but he can see the judge squirm a little in his chair. "Victor something."

"How did things turn out?"

"She found out my real name and made us marry again. I said yes, but only if *she'd* use a false name. Don't know why she agreed. Maybe she thought we'd go again and get it right the third time. Anyway, she went to visit her ma and pa one time, and I took off for Texas." The judge's laugh turns into a coughing fit.

August stares at his glass. One more sip? There was a good chance he'd never drink like this again, so why not?

"You finish that whiskey yet?" the judge asks.

"Half of it," August admits. "Going to have to use your privy."

"Don't bother. Pee off the porch. It's too dark to go wandering around outside."

Later, the judge fetches August a blanket. "Say," he mumbles. "I 'preciate you coming here tonight. That's the most I've had to say about this sorry matter in fifteen years."

"You feel any better?"

"Feel drunk. I'll see how I feel in the morning." He pauses. "You realize we're just two old fools trying to undo the past. Can't be done. But I appreciate you being here, just the same."

. . .

Sleep does not come as easily as August had hoped. The judge's home is surprisingly cold at night, and August prefers a bed to a padded chair. When the thought of pain creeps up on him, he banishes the thought, lest he spend the night awake, fixed on his discomforts. Instead, he thinks back on the day, starting with poor Bullet. He will stop to see Ackerman on the way back to Rhome. Find out how his friend is faring.

Then he thinks of the Aurora graveyard, and in a moment fueled by both fatigue and whiskey, an idea occurs to him. He begins to laugh helplessly, shivering in his chair. He has always had a whimsical side, but surely, he will awaken in the morning with a headache and a rueful memory of this bit of midnight foolishness. Surely, he won't follow through on the idea.

CHAPTER SIXTEEN

Rhome, Texas

Sunday, April 25, 1897

Morning arrives like a shovel to the head. Without help, August hitches Billy to the buckboard and the task is surprisingly difficult—made worse by August's pounding hangover. By the time he finishes, his dirty shirt is soaked in sweat. "I believe I shall quit drinking," he whispers as he climbs onto the buckboard. Peaches the burro watches without comment. Inside the house, the judge is still asleep, and if his volcanic snoring is an indicator, he will not awaken for hours.

Halfway to Ackerman's, the jostling wagon reminds August that he has gone a full day without a dose of laudanum. He considers riding straight to the boarding house, but he is too sick to make the trip without a stop.

When he arrives at Ackerman's, his friend is sitting on a porch chair. He sweats and squints into the sun, slumped over as if he's had a night similar to August's. A piece of sandstone sits at Ackerman's feet, surrounded by tools, including a hammer and chisel.

August pulls close to the front of the house and climbs down from the buckboard, nearly falling on his face. "Hello. May I trouble you for some water?"

"Had a rough night?"

"Yes. The judge insisted I take a sip of his fine whiskey. I must take full blame for the subsequent consumption, however."

Ackerman nods. "I indulged a bit myself last night."

"I wondered," August says.

Ackerman stands—unsteadily—and heads inside. Meanwhile, August tries to mount the porch stairs and finds that the best he can do is to sit on the bottom step. A wave of nausea threatens to empty him. He uses all his concentration to avoid painting Ackerman's porch with whatever remains in his stomach.

Ackerman returns and sets a glass of water down, as if the top step is a table at Hanson's.

August regards the sandstone. It stands eighteen inches tall. The chisel work is clumsy. A shape like a sideways parabola encompasses three tiny circles, one of which is near the apex of the parabola, apart from the other two.

"What's this?" August asks.

"A headstone."

"Some interesting markings you have there."

Ackerman shakes his head, a rueful smile on his lips. "Supposed to be Bullet. That's his nostril, and those are his eyes."

"I see you've put two eyes on one side of his head."

Ackerman looks at the rock as if seeing it for the first time. "It appears that I was not in full possession of my faculties," Ackerman says. "Otherwise, I might have been more anatomically correct."

August tilts his head. "Might also be a comet, about to strike the earth."

Ackerman continues to consider the rock. "It could indeed. I guess I've called down destruction on all of mankind. Whiskey will do that to a man."

August frowns. "A headstone, then?"

"I don't think so. Old Bullet deserves better than that."

August feels another wave of nausea. When it subsides, he sips his water quietly. Ackerman climbs back onto the porch and takes his seat. The dry land around the porch smells hot, like a smelter or a forge. A few hardy weeds grow near the base of Ackerman's house, but the rest of the land is surprisingly devoid of vegetation.

"I want to buy this thing from you," August says at last.

"You're pulling my leg. Are you still drunk from last night?"

August ignores him. "This stone has its charms. For one thing, it will remind me why you chose philosophy over sculpture. But more importantly, I've had an idea." He explains the muse that came to him the previous evening. He finds the urge to laugh is almost overwhelming, and Ackerman's astonished expression only enhances the feeling. When he finishes, Ackerman scratches at his cheek.

"Sounds a touch crazy to me."

"I think that's the draw. You'll have to do some traveling, of course. I imagine Nadine will let you use her buckboard."

"Nadine," Ackerman says. His voice comes out like a sigh.

August purses his lips. "May I ask you something?"

"Sure," he says, but his tone says *I'm not so sure.*

"Does Nadine know how you feel about her?"

Ackerman turns red and looks away. "Did she say something or am I that obvious?"

"She didn't say anything," August says. "There is a certain look on your face when she's around. No harm in it, of course."

Ackerman gazes at his feet. "I think I make her feel uncomfortable."

"There does seem to be some tension between you."

"That, or she's just being Nadine. She can be prickly. Nothing's easy for a woman making her way alone."

"Yes, she can be prickly, but her heart is good." August thinks that Ackerman is a kind man who deserves a companion other than the one interred at the side of the house. "Perhaps she just doesn't know—"

"She knows," Ackerman says. He doesn't lift his gaze from his shoes, curled at the toe and caked in dirt. "I told you before, her heart belongs to someone else." Now he raises his head and meets August's gaze. "I asked her to marry me some years ago." He musters a lopsided grin, as if half his mouth has forgotten to play along. "So, if you planned on matchmaking, you're wasting your time."

"I did not know," August says. "Please pardon me for sticking my nose so far into your business."

. . .

By the time August reaches the boarding house, he is beyond exhausted. It takes him a long time to stable Billy. Though August is naturally resistant to any suggestion that he could use help in any endeavor—a stubbornness borne of pride—he finds himself wishing someone would come to his aid.

Finished with the horse, he finds that Nadine is not in the kitchen, so he is able to make his way to his room without interruption. He removes his clothes, takes a larger dose of his medicine than usual, and fumbles his way under the covers.

When he awakens, it's dark outside. He searches for his clothes but cannot find them. He pulls a shirt and a fresh pair of pants from the dresser. He would have dressed in fresh clothing for church anyway, had he not visited the judge. When he is as presentable as possible, he walks to the kitchen. Only Nadine remains. He has missed dinner.

"Hello," he says. He clears his throat, shocked at how frail he sounds.

"Mr. Simms." She does not smile, but her voice is softer than he is used to.

"I find myself in need of ablutions."

"I thought you might still enjoy a washpot in the bathroom. I've a kettle on."

"Most kind."

"I hope you don't mind, but I checked on you earlier and saw the sorry state of your clothing. I took the liberty of washing them. Were you rolling around in clay?"

She means this as a joke, he realizes, so he does not explain how he helped bury Bullet. Instead, he asks, "I don't suppose there is anything left from the evening meal? I'm uncustomarily hungry." No wonder. He has gone the entire day without a bite of food.

"Mr. Chambers prevents the waste of food, but I can find something for you. Wash up and I'll fix something." She blushes. "We were interrupted in our conversation several days ago. I would like to finish if you have the strength."

"I should like that very much. But I worry that others will repeat the interruption."

Nadine snorts. "Not tonight. Misters MacGregor and Chambers are suddenly best of friends. They took the buckboard into town to Hanson's for some ale."

"Wonder of wonders."

"You have yourself to blame," Nadine says, leading him to the bathroom with a kettle of hot water. "You seem to have a bonding effect on others."

Cleaning up takes longer than he wishes. The water in the washpot is cold by the time he finishes. He dresses again, carries the pan to the porch, and tosses the water into the yard. Nadine is nowhere in sight, so he wanders around the corner to find her sitting where Christy used to sit. She has a plate of food in her lap and a glass of tea at the side of his chair. When he sits down, she passes the plate over—a slice of fresh bread, half a chicken breast, and a wedge of pie. "Peaches," she says, and August thinks of Judge Proctor's burro.

She waits to talk until he finishes eating. As hungry as he is, he can only eat half the pie wedge.

She asks, "Was the pie acceptable?"

"It was wonderful."

"Last season's canned peaches," she says. "I'm clearing the pantry out. I hope we get some summer visitors so I can afford to restock."

"Your pie is as good as any I've had," August says. "Did I taste nutmeg?"

"Yes," she says, surprised. "Was it too much?"

"Absolutely not." He sets the plate and fork by the side of his chair. "Now. If I recall correctly, you asked what I remembered from the night your father died."

"Yes," she says. The word comes out, but her jaw does not seem to move.

"What do *you* remember?"

"Not much," she says. Her voice is a terse whisper. "My mother was hysterical, of course. Townspeople found my father on the road home and brought him here. He was already gone by then. They carried him into the house and put him on the table so he wouldn't bleed on the upholstered furniture, I suppose. I tried to go to him, but they kept me away. They said I was too young for a sight like that." She scowls. "Idiots. I was sixteen years old."

August nods absently. He remembers all of it.

"I don't recall you being there, sir," she says. "Not that I would. There were so many people in the house. All those people, and no one would talk to me. I kept asking what happened and they kept shooing me away. So much shouting and wailing, and not a word for me."

"So, you went outside and sat on the porch."

"Yes," she says, astonished. "How do you know that?"

"A man came out and sat next to you on the steps."

Nadine turns in her chair, searching his face. The moon slides behind a cloud, so the far side of the porch is dark as charcoal.

"I was clean-shaven then, and stout. Age has whittled me down some."

"You?"

"I wasn't sure what to say to a young woman who'd just lost her father. There are no appropriate words, really. So, I just sat there with you."

"Mr. Simms." Her breath is halfway between a sigh and a moan.

"August. I would prefer August."

"August, then. Yes, I remember now. You said *nothing*, and that was the only right thing. Your presence was the best comfort you could give me. After a while—" Her voice cracks.

"You put your head on my shoulder. No small feat, as I sat with some distance between us, as befits a gentleman and a young woman." He sips his tea. "I recall that you ran the boarding house while your mother convalesced. I know she died the following year—perhaps of a broken heart. You ran the family business alone, did you not?"

Nadine's voice has become a whisper. "That night, your shirt smelled of tobacco." She is remembering.

"Not my tobacco," August says. "The other men who boarded with you were fond of their cigars. Cigar smoke clings to everything."

"I'm so sorry I didn't recognize you. You wear a goatee now."

"My wife did not appreciate whiskers back then," he says. "They irritated her skin. If I wanted a kiss, I needed to present a smooth face."

They sit quietly. August scans the dark field for a sign of the deer that comes to visit now and then, but he can't see much beyond the porch rail. "Do you remember the rest of the story?" he asks.

"I'm not sure. To what are you referring?"

"My wife was ill. She died at the end of the summer. Three days later, as a matter of fact." He knows what he wants to tell her, but his voice nearly betrays him. He sips his tea before continuing. "When she died, I sat at her bedside for most of the afternoon and evening. Then, someone took her away in a wagon. I don't recall who. Summer in Texas does horrible things to a corpse. There was no graveyard in Rhome, so they sent her to Aurora and buried her the next day. Several of your boarders took me to and from the funeral." He stops and shakes his head. "But that was later. The day she died, I went out to the porch and sat in this very chair. Is it the same chair? Well, in this spot anyway. The sun was down, as it is now, and I sat there trying to decide."

Nadine is silent now.

"Then I felt a hand on my shoulder. You crossed in front and sat in the chair you're in now—in that very spot—and you took my hand. We sat there for a while, and then you stood up and said something about the work you had waiting for you, and you scurried off. But by then, I'd decided to live."

"I don't remember that."

"Of course not. Acts of kindness come naturally to you. They are only remarkable to those around you."

"There are some who find no virtue in me at all."

"You're speaking of Natalie? I take it you had a row."

Her voice hardens again. "You've probably wondered where her father is."

August does not answer, but of course he's wondered.

"I ran the boarding house after my father's death, as you said. My mother's role was limited to criticizing my choices. I did not always listen to her advice, and it cost me. One day in the spring following my father's death, I was supposed to make a supply run, but the day got away from me and the sun was down. I was young. Young people think they are immortal. I recall my mother taking me to task for going out in the dark alone. She repeated herself when I came back, bruised and bloodied. Nine months later, I had Natalie."

Anger rushes through August, but he does not comment. This is her story. He will not interrupt her to tell her what a foul tragedy she is relating. Even in the dark, he can tell she is looking directly at him.

"He was a railroad man. He followed me back from Hanson's. I remember thinking that it was kind of him not to steal all the supplies I'd purchased, but when we unloaded the buckboard, the bacon was gone. *That* made me cry." She sniffles. "I won't have them in my house. Railroad men, I mean."

August closes his eyes and concentrates on her voice, which shifts in turns from soft and vulnerable to hard and sardonic. "What an amazing life you've led. The things you've survived—"

"I've spent most of my life in Rhome, Texas." Her tone is a mixture of regret and amusement. "Hardly a life of adventure."

"No two days alike, I'd imagine. And now, trouble with Pastor Allen?"

Silence. Has he overstepped himself? "It's all right if you don't want to talk about it."

When she speaks again, her voice is detached. She has not left her chair yet, but in a moment she will do so. "I've enjoyed reminiscing with you, but I believe I've indulged in enough soul baring for one evening." She rises, gathers his plate and utensils, and walks to the corner of the porch. Her steps are steady and deliberate. "Thank you for your kind thoughts. Good night, August." Then she is gone.

CHAPTER SEVENTEEN

Rhome, Texas
Monday, April 26, 1897

August wakes to the sound of pounding on the door. "One moment," he calls. "I'm getting dressed." A glance through the window tells him it's not yet dawn. He pulls on his Sunday pants and shirt, tugs at his beard, pats his hair into place, and cracks the door.

Nadine's voice matches her stricken expression. "She's gone! Is she here? In your room?"

"Who?"

"Natalie!" She stands, lantern in hand. The light illuminates her ghostly face from below. Worry lines ripple her forehead.

August opens the door wide. "Why on earth would she be in my room?"

"I thought she might come to talk to you. *Everyone* talks to you. I thought she might—" She breaks off with a groan.

August steps back. "Come in."

Nadine grips the door frame. "I have to find her. She's not in the house."

"Have you checked everywhere?"

"Yes, yes. This was my last hope." She grimaces. "I'm a madwoman, waking everyone."

"Do you know when she left?"

"No. Yes, sometime in the night. It's not safe after dark!" She bites her lip, and August wonders if she might break skin.

"Try to calm down. Tell me what happened. When you finish, I'll go looking for her."

Nadine takes a tentative step forward and then stands in place, swaying slightly. "I need to find her—"

"No, you do not. If she returns, she needs her mother here, waiting for her."

"I'm supposed to wait?"

"Yes. Exactly that." He places a hand on the dresser to brace himself as he slips his stocking feet into his shoes, one at a time. Nadine waits, lantern in hand. "Now, tell me what's happening so I know what I'm getting myself into."

"We argued. She was angry. *So* angry. But I never thought she'd pack up and leave."

"She took her things?" August asks.

"Her clothes are gone."

August nods, thinking. "Do you have any idea where she might go?" he asks. "Perhaps to Bill Ackerman's?"

"She's never been there, as far as I know. She might, though. Do you think so?"

"Hard to say. I don't know what's happened, so I'm just guessing."

Nadine's face hardens. "I suppose I must tell you, then." She crosses the room and sits at the end of the bed, her hands in her lap. She is silent at first, a sour expression darkening her face. When she finally speaks, her voice borders on a cold whisper. "I'll warn you in advance that I don't really care to hear your opinion in this matter. You may judge me all you like but keep it to yourself."

"As you wish," August says.

"If, after hearing this, you decide to move out, I won't say a word to stop you. Simply pack your things and leave. Your assessment has no particular value to me."

"Nadine, *please.*"

She looks away.

"What are you afraid of?"

She scowls. "I'm not afraid."

"Then trust me," August says. He pulls open the dresser drawer and removes the bottle of laudanum. He drinks from the bottle, not bothering to measure a dose. Some of the liquid dribbles from the corner of his mouth. He wipes it away with the back of his shirtsleeve. "There," he says. "It will take me a few minutes to hitch Billy to the buckboard, but I'm nearly on my way. Let's not waste time."

Her expression melts, giving way to teary eyes and trembling lips. She runs a hand through her hair and grabs the ends in her fist. "She saw something she shouldn't have."

She is silent for a moment, so he says, "Perhaps a little more detail."

"My friend, Abigail."

"Bose's sister."

"We were childhood friends. She cleans rooms here on Fridays."

"I saw her here."

"Yes, well, Natalie saw us exchange a kiss." Natalie looks away again. After a moment, she adds, "It was not a chaste kiss."

August does not immediately comprehend. When he does, he blushes. "I think I understand. Are you saying—"

"Yes." Nadine's frown returns. "We were playmates and then, friends. Confidantes. Then my father was murdered, and her father was murdered, and we shared something deeper. I doubt you can understand what that means." Nadine stares into her lap. "After I was attacked, Abby was my sole comfort." Now, she raises her gaze. Her voice is matter of fact. "Eventually, the friendship became love."

"Did you explain that to Natalie?"

"I did not."

August nods. "And Pastor Allen? How does he fit in all of this?"

"Natalie saw fit to confide in him. He reacted as one would expect. He quoted some scripture, packed his bag, and left." Now she looks directly at him—a challenge of sorts. "I suppose you regard this sort of thing as a sin."

"The Bible seems to," he says. "But we are all sinners, and sins come in varying degrees. Each night, Mr. Chambers empties your serving plates into his stomach. The Bible says gluttony is a sin. I think your particular sin must rank between Mr. Chambers' appetite and failing to excuse oneself for a belch."

She stares at him as if she does not understand. "Let me be clearer," August continues. "I cannot believe that God regards genuine love to be much of a sin." Outside, the sun is beginning to show its first rays. Given what August has learned, he will check the schoolhouse where church services are held. Perhaps the pastor is sleeping there, having left the boarding house. "I've traveled all over the world, Nadine. This sort of attraction is not unknown. Nor, for that matter, is a mixing of the races."

"But we're in *Texas*."

"Yes. We are in Texas. And for Texas, you've taken the cake, assuming there is a prize for providing the largest number of people an opportunity for outrage."

Nadine's expression changes again. Now, she is angry. "I don't care what they think."

"It's no one else's business," he agrees, pulling at his goatee. "But I wonder. Who else knows about this?"

"Bose. Bill Ackerman—"

"Bill knows?" *Of course he does.* He'd said, *her heart belongs to someone else.*

"Years ago, Bill expressed some romantic notions, and in a moment of frankness, I told him the truth. I've regretted it ever since."

"You needn't have. He's kept your secrets."

"Well, someone has said something." She sighs. "Rocks keep hitting my door."

"One I saw had a note attached. What did it say?"

Nadine is fuming now. "Every Friday, Abby comes here. And every Wednesday, I go to her house. It's the *only* time we have together. A year or so ago, someone asked me why I go to that side of town. I made up a lie. Said I was teaching Abigail to read." She snorts and shakes her head. "That girl can quote Shakespeare. That's a truth they wouldn't believe. But a lie? They swallow it with a smile."

"The note?" August prompts.

"Said I spend too much time with that—" She stops short. "I won't use that word."

"That's bad, but it doesn't say much about your affections," August says. "If they knew more, they'd likely say more." He shakes his head. "And Bose knows, too?"

"Yes, and he threw a fit about it. Made a lot of noise, like men do. But he loves his sister too much to stay angry. I'm a different matter. He won't talk to me."

"He strikes me as a man who doesn't say much to anyone."

Nadine looks back down at her lap. "I think Natalie hates me now."

"That is nonsense," August says. He walks to the door. "I'm going to go fetch her. If she comes back while I'm gone, tell her what you told me. Your explanation is heartfelt. Give her a chance to show what kind of person she's going to be."

"Where will you go?" Nadine asks.

"I'll start with a visit to Pastor Allen. She might be staying at the schoolhouse, or he might have arranged for some well-meaning family to give her shelter."

"What will you tell her when you find her?" Nadine's face is once again stricken.

"I'll let her do most of the talking," August says. "If I were a gambler, I'd bet she's already looking for a reason to come home."

. . .

The sun is up. August rides the buckboard to the Prairie Point Schoolhouse, considering what he might say to the pastor. The man enjoys verbal sparring, and he arms himself with scripture. August is reminded of his own father—a Presbyterian minister in Ohio. Firm in his opinions. Married to the letter of the law. A good person, in the sense that he was internally consistent. August never once detected an element of hypocrisy in the man. August owed much to his father for his knowledge of the Bible. Nonetheless, they were not close, and when he died, there had been no great sense of loss. Instead, a melancholy regret for missed opportunities and connections that were never made.

He finds Pastor Allen inside the schoolhouse, stacking the congregation's limited number of hymnals. His rumpled appearance gives credence to August's suspicions—he's taken up residence in the schoolhouse. One look from the pastor tells him what he needs to know. "She's here," August says.

"Yes, and she's better for it. First Corinthians 15:33. *Do not be deceived. Evil companionships corrupt good morals.*"

"True," says August. He eases himself into a chair and breathes a pained sigh. "One must always be aware of bad influences."

Pastor Allen regards him carefully.

"I've come to speak with Natalie."

"Are you acting as an emissary for her mother?"

"I am," August says.

"You are uninformed, then. I regret to tell you—"

"I'm fully informed," August says.

"What say you in this matter, then?"

August gives him a thin-lipped smile. "Sins have been committed."

"Indeed," Pastor Allen says. He reaches up to pat his oiled hair into place. "Leviticus 18:22. *Thou shalt not lie with mankind, as with womankind: it is abomination.*"

August gives him a slow, careful nod. "I am reminded of those two cities of the plain, struck to cinders by an angry God."

The pastor places a hand over his heart. "Deuteronomy 29:23. *The whole land is brimstone, salt, and burning; it is not sown, nor does it bear, nor does any grass grow there.*" His voice sounds a warning. "There, but for our efforts and the grace of God, lies the fate of our township."

The school's interior is cool. For now, the room has the studied peace of a library. The pastor has arranged chairs in rows. At the head of the room, a raised platform and the teacher's desk stand in for an altar.

"I was thinking," August says, his voice steady, "of the *other* sins of Sodom and Gomorrah. Ezekiel 16:49-50. *This was the guilt of your sister Sodom: she and her daughters had pride, excess of food, and prosperous ease, but did not aid the poor and needy. They were haughty and did abominable things before me.*"

Pastor Allen tilts his head. "Your knowledge of scripture is impressive." There is a hint of genuine admiration in his voice.

"The other sins," August repeats. "The cities on the plains were inhospitable to their fellows. Much like a community that fails to embrace all of its members. Nadine Martin has been a good neighbor for decades, and if loose gossip—"

"The townspeople have a right to know," Pastor Allen says.

August's heart sinks. "Surely, you've told no one."

"They have a right to know," the pastor repeats.

August's worst fears have been realized. For a moment, his anger bests him. "And the people of Sodom and Gomorrah were haughty and judgmental—"

Pastor Allen slaps the chair in front of him for emphasis. "The Bible is the word of God. It is the *law.*"

"Then follow it, sir. *Honor thy mother and father*—a commandment. Yet, you counseled a girl on the cusp of adulthood to turn her back on her mother." August rises from the pew. "Did you not?"

"I did not!" The pastor says, but his face says otherwise. Had the man not considered the meaning of his actions? Quite possible. To do so was a common human foible.

August begins walking toward the altar. At that end of the room, two doors lead out, one to each side. "There are two kinds of Christians, Pastor. One kind follows the letter of the law, using scripture as a solicitor would, never thinking beyond the bare words. They do not take the intent of the law or the context of the situation into account, which is why final judgement is properly reserved for the Lord." He takes a gasping breath. Long sentences wind him. "As for the other kind of Christian, he reads the Holy Book for wisdom, prays, and above all else, soothes his anger with God's love." August stops moving and glances back over his shoulder. "I will watch with interest to see which kind of Christian *you* are."

"You presume much," Pastor Allen says. His voice is choked.

"For that alone, I beg your forgiveness." August points to the altar. "Left, or right?"

"Pardon?"

"Is she in the room to the left or to the right?"

The pastor stares without speaking. Just as August is ready to give up hope for an answer, Pastor Allen says, "To the right."

The room on the right faces away from the sun, so he doesn't see her at first. Instead, he sees a small bookcase stuffed with primers, a pair of brooms with straw worn down to the binding, and a table with one leg askew. When his eyes adjust to the shadows, he spots her in the corner, sitting on the floor, knees drawn up, arms wrapped around her legs. She looks at him with puffy eyes. "I knew it was you. I heard you arguing."

"The pastor is fond of debate." He sidesteps in order to reach the wall, where he can hold himself in place without losing his balance. "You look very sad."

"My world is crumbling to pieces," she says, and she begins to sob.

"Your world is quite intact." Reaching into his pocket, he pulls out a handkerchief. Reluctantly removing his free hand from the wall, he crosses to her and hands her the linen. "Dry your eyes."

"She hates me now."

"That is nonsense."

"Why did you come for me? Why didn't she come herself?"

"Because one of us had to be there in case you came home. Come on, now." He holds out his hand.

"You don't know what happened!"

"Yes, I do."

"But the pastor says—"

"The pastor is a man. The same as any other man. You would do well not to believe everything they say. What does your heart tell you?"

"I don't know."

"You have to decide." August keeps his hand extended. "The pastor has not been silent, and I fear there will be repercussions. Will you face what's coming on your own, or will you join family and friends?"

"What's coming? What do you mean?"

"Trouble is knocking. Your mother will need your help and support."

Only a few seconds more pass before she takes his hand.

CHAPTER EIGHTEEN

Rhome, Texas
Monday, April 26, 1897

Dinner is a somber affair. The mood simmers like the pot roast Nadine prepared. A knock at the door changes the meal's temperament. Bill Ackerman arrives, hat in hand, inviting himself to the table. He sits in the pastor's former spot and helps himself to the leftovers that Mr. Chambers had been eyeing. "I wondered what Nadine's cooking was like," Bill explains. "August here is getting fat—sorry to say it—so the food must be wonderful."

"You've had dinner here before, Bill," Nadine says.

"Not for years. You've had time to improve your cooking."

Nadine frowns, but everyone else at the table smiles or chuckles. Even Natalie musters a grin as Ackerman tastes the pot roast.

"Well?" Nadine asks. "Was it worth the wait?"

Ackerman considers the question as if he were Bob Cratchit with a mouth full of bread pudding. "A triumph," he says at last. Laughter, this time, and the dinner table is a brighter place.

The evening sun angles in through the window, putting a warm copper glow on the walls and faces. The smell of fresh biscuits and roast gives August a sense of great comfort, and he thinks again that he has chosen the perfect place to finish his life. If he'd had children, he might have chosen differently. His only sibling,

Catherine, died in 1845 from the Black Cholera, and she'd been childless. He'd already said his goodbyes to any friends he hadn't outlived. This table, these people, would be the only family he would have in his remaining days.

"Nadine," Ackerman says. "There's a little bit left here. You should sit down and join us." The other men at the table voice their approval, and after some head shaking and hand waving, she says, "All right. Just this once."

After dinner, MacGregor and Chambers wander off on an evening walk, and August sits with Bill on the far side of the porch, leaving Nadine and Natalie alone in the kitchen. "Are those two talking to each other?" Ackerman asks.

"I assume so," August says. "I've left them alone to work things out." He glances at his friend. "How did you know they had a disagreement?"

"People are talking."

"What did you hear?"

"Enough," Ackerman says. "I suppose you know everything now?"

"One can never be sure," August says. "But I know about Natalie's father, and I know about Abigail."

Ackerman nods. "Hope you don't hold it against me for not telling you."

August says, "I admire a man who will not betray a trust."

A breath of wind rustles the saw grass. The open field looks deceptively flat and serene, but he knows better. He's walked this field. Underneath the green, rocks and holes pit the landscape. No good for a hike or a ride in the dark. Too many pitfalls.

"Don't think less of her," Ackerman says.

"Of course not. But I do think she's put herself in a rough spot." August strokes his goatee. "She hates the railroad folk—"

"With good reason."

August shrugs. "Yes, with good reason. If word gets around about Abigail, they'll have ammunition to use against her. For one thing, they won't recommend the boarding house to travelers."

Ackerman snorts. "No, they sure won't."

"Things could get nastier than that."

"I know." Ackerman touches his blackened eye. "This little addition to my face happened because they didn't much like Nadine's friendship with Abigail. Apparently, people have been speculating. Now they have assurances, thanks to our pastor, who carried his pulpit mouth into Hanson's for a congregation of drunks."

"How many people did he tell?" August asks.

"All of 'em,"

"The storm might pass," August says. "I think I'll hike into town and check the temperature. Monday night? Maybe folks will be in the mood to chat."

"There are some railroad boys holding over. Some of them board at the stable, since they're not welcome here. Could be rough. Want some company?"

"No, I don't think so. You need to save face—what's left of it."

"Ha. You're a funny man for somebody with one foot in the grave."

"Maybe," August says, patting Ackerman's arm. "But I think I have a better hold on my temper than you do."

"That's the truth," Ackerman says. "All right, then. I'll sit here and wait for you. If you don't get back, I'll come looking with a shovel in my hand."

"To defend me or bury me?"

Ackerman nods.

.   .   .

The tables at Hanson's are full. Though the others are drinking whiskey, Hanson has a Dr. Pepper waiting for him. August takes his drink to a table with an open chair, having spotted someone he knows. "Wilson, isn't it?"

The man smiles. He's drinking coffee, though it might carry a splash of something else. "August Simms, right?"

August sits. "Yes." He looks around the room. "A lot of railroad men here tonight."

"The locomotive needs some work," he says. "We're waiting." He takes a sip from his cup. "It's normal. You'd be amazed to learn how seldom we stay on schedule." He sets his cup down and surveys the room. "Most of these boys are out of Pueblo, Colorado. Rode in from the Denver and New Orleans railroad, hauling coal from Franceville."

"Amazing how the world links up by rail," August says. "Used to be, you needed to follow the rivers."

"Yes."

"Someday, we won't need rails. We'll fly where we need to go."

"How will that work?" he asks. His smile and his blue eyes betray a hint of amusement.

"I suspect that major cities will establish air hubs, linked to other hubs so that the spokes cover everywhere, from coast to coast."

"Hubs?"

"Aeroportals, if you will."

Wilson takes another sip. "First, someone will have to design an aeroship."

"Ahh," August says. "I'm fairly certain that has already happened."

Wilson's smile spreads across his face. "Some here would disagree." He nods in the direction of the other men in the room. "The general consensus here is that the sightings across Texas are a prank. Some railroad boys have even taken credit."

"Why do that?"

"To break up the day, I suppose. We work long hours. Twenty-six-hour shifts or longer. Some of these boys are gandy dancers—"

"Pardon?"

"Section hands. They maintain the track."

"Which ones?"

Wilson lifts an eyebrow. "Most of the time, you can tell them by their race. The Irish lay the rails and the Mexicans maintain them."

"And the native-born?" August asks.

"Conductors. Engineers. Yardmen, too. Now, their lot is difficult. Coupling and uncoupling cars is hard, dangerous work. Lose a finger or a hand in a blink. Sometimes a leg or foot. The bigger companies have railway surgeons with their own hospital cars. They can rush help to the scene of an accident."

"That sounds very practical."

Wilson shakes his head. "The boys don't like it. They have their wages garnished to pay the surgeon's salaries. The traditional medical doctors don't think much of the railway surgeons, either."

"What do you think of them?" August asks.

"They're good with prosthetics, I can say that. Quick with an amputation, too."

August gives a thoughtful nod. "I saw much the same in the war. What looks like butchery can, in fact, be skill and experience, given a particular kind of injury."

"An apt comparison," Wilson says. "I read a quote from a congressman in the papers. Cabot Lodge, I think. He said, *they suffer as if they were fighting a war.* That stuck with me. The men in Washington seldom focus on the plight of the working man. Lodge is an exception." He glances at the others in the room. "Railroading will break a man's back." His gaze flicks from man to man. "Ten men here. Odds are, half of them will die on the job, or quit before the rails can get them."

"Those are harrowing odds, indeed."

Wilson nods. "Endless labor for those who mind the track. As for the train crews, they are seldom at home. When they lay over in a small town like this one, they've nothing to do but drink or fight. If they've wives, they lose them to the distance. It's a single man's profession, for certain." He pushes his coffee cup aside and sits back.

"Are you married?" August asks.

"I was, once."

August glances at his Dr. Pepper. He likes the sweet taste, but it's the evening. Lately, anything other than water gives him bloat. If Hanson had charged for water, he'd have bought a glass of that instead. "You appear to have escaped serious injury. What do you do for the railroad?"

"I'm an engineer."

"You drive one of those locomotives? I envy you, sir."

"No, no. I'm a mechanical engineer. I bring physics, mathematics, and a knowledge of physical materials to bear on special projects."

"Interesting. You must find talk about the airships to be most intriguing."

Wilson narrows his gaze, and for a long time, he is silent. When he leans forward, hands on the table, his voice is barely a whisper. "There is a secret history, my friend. A history that tells the tale of wars and their real beginnings, and of undisclosed knowledge and inventions that never see the light of day. It's a story of money, and power, and lost opportunities." He sits back, and when he speaks again, he no longer whispers. "Take the impending war with Spain. Do you wonder what machinations are going on behind the scenes, and whose pockets are about to be lined?"

"I pray there will be no war."

"You strike me as a man of science, not a man of faith."

August does not answer, because he finds value in both.

"I will not ask you, then, to take on faith the notion of a fleet of airships, crafted by a secret organization of engineers and inventors, dedicated to exploring the skies."

"I would not doubt its existence," August says. "But I wonder. Why would they not seek publicity for their achievements?"

"For fear of their failures," Wilson says.

At that moment, a man enters Hanson's. He is a small, scruffy fellow with a cap in hand. His bib overalls are covered in dark stains, perhaps grease. He draws a long sleeve across his forehead and says, "We're ready to roll."

Half the men in Hanson's hoot their displeasure, and one throws a piece of bread at the man who is clearly used to such abuse, given his curt wave of dismissal. "Come along or be left behind. Makes no never mind to me."

"Fuck yourself," one of the men shouts.

"Already had your mother," the scruffy one says, pivoting on his boot heel and rushing out the door.

Wilson shakes his head. "Leaving at this hour? Well then." He offers a hand. "As before, I find you an interesting man. Aeroportals? What an imagination you have, sir."

August takes the hand and shakes it. "I enjoyed our conversation. Good luck with your special projects."

"Perhaps we'll speak again."

August almost says, *no, probably not. I'm dying.* Instead, he says, "I hope so. I will press you for more on this secret history. As it happens, I've secrets of my own."

"I would not doubt it," Wilson says, echoing August's earlier sentiments.

CHAPTER NINETEEN

Rhome, Texas
Tuesday, April 27, 1897

Ackerman stays overnight, taking the pastor's old room. There are still two empty rooms upstairs, and Nadine needs to fill at least one of them to stay even with her expenses. Ackerman insists on paying for the night, despite Nadine's protests. August knows this because he hears the altercation from inside his room. Two old friends, bickering. A good sound.

August takes a larger dose of laudanum than usual. He is less concerned about supply since meeting the doctor in Rhome. He does not like the man, who seems a self-important sort, but access to the medicine is critical. August dreads physical pain. In fact, if the pain of cancer exceeds the capabilities of the medicine, he will take his two-shot derringer from his travel trunk and solve the problem.

That he would consider suicide so casually does not surprise him. He's lived for fifteen years without his beloved wife—a grudging responsibility that is coming to an end. He has no doubt that he's fulfilled his obligation to his creator by traveling the final portion of his life alone.

The subject of sin brings a memory. During the war, his men took a prisoner from the rebel army. News of the atrocities at Fort Pillow left them in a vengeful mood. They tossed a rope over an elm branch and strung the rebel up two inches off the ground so that he toed the dirt, struggling for air. When August came upon the scene, he found angry soldiers brandishing torches, righteous in their hatred, and a Judas goat facing flames for the sin of slavery. August drew his pistol and shot the man dead. Murder? Perhaps. But the rebel's death was foregone, and August would not allow the kind of suffering his men had in mind. He did not reprimand them, these soldiers under his command, so he was allowed to walk away with his life.

Suicide may indeed be a sin, but like Nadine's transgressions, it is a minor one. If God on high judges, He does not do so consulting a ledger.

The morning sun brings clarity. Staring through the window, August realizes that if Nadine is in danger, Abigail's situation is even more precarious. There are spare rooms at the boarding house. Someone must fetch Abigail from Rhome and bring her here. Might Chambers or MacGregor balk at this plan? He does not think so, nor does he care if they do. As for losing future business, Nadine has money coming that she does not know about—money that will rectify any financial consequences.

After breakfast, August asks Bill to accompany him to Hanson's. They walk the dirt road together. Ackerman moves slowly, pacing himself to August's progress. A yellow-breasted chat squeaks and chuckles from its perch in the scrub. Ackerman tries to answer back, but he is not adept with birdcalls.

"I wanted to discuss something with you," August says. "My time is coming to an end—"

"You seem mighty quick to jump in a hole," Ackerman says.

August snorts a laugh. "You have a way with words." He stops walking. Ackerman takes another two steps before stopping as well. "Bill, I've written to my lawyer. He will deliver a bank draft to Nadine after my death. It's not a fortune, but it will be enough to repair the boarding house and put aside something extra for emergencies. I've placed instructions for you in an envelope in my travel trunk. It has the details of the transaction, should something go wrong. Will you see to things for me?"

"Of course. But we don't need to talk about this now—"

"Yes, we do."

"You could last another year—"

"To put my mind at ease, Bill."

Ackerman's expression draws long, but he nods his agreement.

"In the meantime, there is this." He hands over a small pouch.

Ackerman opens it up and shakes his head. The pouch contains some gold coins and large denomination bills. "No—"

"Yes. It's not much. But I've seen your farm. You might have another crop like this year's."

"What crop?"

"My point exactly. Call this a grant. You'll be able to continue your study of mankind. You might even buy yourself another horse."

"Not likely." Ackerman closes the pouch.

"There are strings, of course. There's the matter of your sculpture." He reaches into his pocket and pulls out a handful of fused nuggets—the mystery metal from atop his dresser. He'd told Natalie, truthfully, that he didn't know their composition. Certainly, nothing currently in production. "Here are the metal bits I mentioned. Place some at the gravesite—"

"And some in Judge Proctor's well. I hope he doesn't shoot me."

"I hope so as well," August says, straight-faced.

"Tell me again why you want me to do this."

August considers the question. "If I say that life has moments of horror, you will agree." He is thinking of the war. Ackerman might well be thinking of Bullet's funeral. "There are sad moments, funny moments, fear, drudgery, and excitement. Love, if you are lucky. All those things make up a life." He pauses. "Whimsey, too. This is my little jest. A goodbye with a smile."

"I'm not sure anyone will get the joke."

August laughs. "My jokes are funny because they make *me* laugh."

Ackerman shakes his head. "Crazy old man." He grips the pouch. "Thanks for the money. I don't want you to think I don't appreciate it."

August puts a hand on the taller man's shoulder. "There's more to discuss. I am worried about Nadine's friend, Abigail."

"I thought the same thing this morning."

"Because she earns her money as a domestic, we might convince her to relocate here. I believe we should ask Nadine her opinion on the matter."

"Not sure how the town would take that, given the rumors."

"Offering quarters to a servant is common enough. Besides, the safety of the women comes first. Shall we ask to borrow Nadine's buckboard and see to Abigail?"

"I thought we were going to Hanson's."

"That was a prevarication."

"You are a scandalous old man." Ackerman says. He turns back for the boarding house. "Let's get to it. Nadine ought to agree out of hand, but lately, she's been—"

"Prickly," August finishes.

.   .   .

Rhome's colored community is situated in a rough semicircle around the large cabin used for church services. Homes vary in size and construction, from small shacks plastered with tar paper to larger frame-and-plank houses. Abigail's house is one of the latter. Her father was a handyman, so the house has a shingled roof and timber-framed construction that looks sturdier than the surrounding homes. A wooden bucket sits at the edge of the porch, filled with blooming Texas bluebells and buttercups.

Abigail steps onto the porch to greet them when the wagon pulls in. "Mr. Simms? Is something wrong, sir?" Not *suh*, but *sir*. Her voice is precise and melodic.

August tries to speak but realizes, to his embarrassment, that he does not have the proper words. She blinks her amber eyes and smiles, hands folded in front, her back straight as a rake. Her beauty and her regal bearing is the problem. The message he's come to deliver is coarse and inappropriate. He stands silent.

Ackerman comes to the rescue. "We think you're in danger, Miss Abigail."

She tilts her head. "How so?"

August swallows. "There's been gossip about your friendship with Nadine," he says. "People being who and what they are . . ." His voice trails off.

Ackerman jumps back in. "Nadine says staying at the boarding house will save you travel time, since you are employed there."

"Yes, I am. *One* day a week. I have other obligations."

"I suspect she needs additional help at the boarding house," August says. "We men are a handful."

Abigail's shoulders shake as she stifles a laugh. "That much is true." She purses her lips. "I believe you've come here as a kindness, gentlemen, and I am grateful. But this is my home. My things are here. I am determined to stay."

"I don't blame you. Your home is lovely," August says. "But there have been threats."

"Threats?"

"Rocks with notes tied to them. Thrown at the house." August glances at Ackerman, who seems surprised. He didn't know.

"My poor house has suffered rocks in the past. Yet here I am."

August shakes his head. "You don't understand. The gossip has changed."

"Mr. Simms. I am cognizant of the danger to any person of color. How could I be otherwise? Nonetheless, this is my home, and I will stay here."

Ackerman toes the ground with his boot, hand shoved in his pockets. After a moment, he looks up and says, "They know about you and Nadine."

Her smile disappears. When she speaks again, her chin is raised. Her voice is firm. "If I am to live in the world, gentlemen, I must believe in the basic goodness of men. I am a God-fearing woman. I live a humble life. I have been a good neighbor. I am a threat to no one. Should anyone wish to do me harm, they will find me resolute."

August scans the house behind her. The wood joints—carved and pegged—show marvelous workmanship. "As I said, your house is lovely. Well-constructed."

"My father built it with his two hands. He was a craftsman."

"Your father was a good man. The town lynched him anyway."

Abigail's eyes seem to catch fire, and she lets a scowl take her expression. "Mr. Simms! Did you imagine I'd forgotten?"

August shakes his head in defeat. "I am sorry," he says. "I have overstepped. I ask your forgiveness." He must think of a way to rescue this mission. "But Miss Williams? May I ask a favor of you?"

She does not answer. She stands above him on the porch, arms folded. Waiting.

"Please tell your brother what I've told you. He's a smart man. Trust his counsel. If you reconsider your decision, you do not need a second invitation to join us."

Abigail Williams gazes off in the distance and then smiles. Frowns do not seem natural to her, for she keeps losing hers. "Thank you for your visit. You must excuse me, gentlemen. The day's chores are waiting."

They have been dismissed.

. . .

"Do you think she'll talk to Bose?"

"I do," August says. "She didn't say so directly, but I believe she will." The road seems bumpier on the way back, and he is not looking forward to Nadine's disappointment. "Miss Williams is a proud woman."

"Pride's a sin," Ackerman says.

"Not when the pride is earned."

The boarding house looms ahead. August looks at the building differently as the buckboard approaches. The ground cover is clear in front of the porch, but the field to the side of the house—the field he's been gazing at each night from his seat on the porch—is overgrown. No tree cover other than the motte of dark trees in the distance, which is a good thing.

The house can be approached on all sides. There are no fences.

The second story is recessed from the ground floor, ringed by a sub-roof, leaving blind spots along the full perimeter of the boarding house. The ground floor has plenty of windows, except for the west side—the back of the house. Only two doors—one in front and one in back. But those windows!

The tiny barn where Billy and the buckboard spend the night stands fifty feet from the back side of the house. Good cover for any approach. Perhaps, if August and the others play possum, they can marshal their forces at the rear of the house.

But what resistance can they offer? He has a two-shot derringer in his travel trunk, meant for point-blank range. He would not trust its accuracy beyond ten feet. Did Nadine keep a gun? He certainly hadn't seen one. He would ask.

He stands at the back of the house, staring up at the second story. The lack of westside windows is good for keeping a cooler house in the summer. Bad for observing any hostile advance. Ackerman follows him at a distance, watching with a curious expression.

"Can I ask what you're doing?"

"Sure," August says. "Looking at the house."

"More than that," Ackerman says. "You have a funny expression on your face."

"Ah. My soldier's face."

Ackerman frowns.

"I'm looking at the house with an eye for defense. One must hope for the best and prepare for the worst."

"And?"

August shakes his head. "The boarding house is indefensible."

CHAPTER TWENTY

Rhome, Texas
Tuesday, April 27, 1897
Ackerman heads back home after conferring with August, who intends to revisit Hanson's in the evening. If he's lucky, there will be fewer railroad men and more townsfolk. He will engage them in discussion. Perhaps argue in favor of their better angels. If things become heated, he will conjure some verbal jiggery-pokery. He is an adept.

Nadine is understandably concerned about Abigail. August promises to pay her a second visit if what he hears at Hanson's gives him pause. He is reminded of his two trips to Judge Proctor years earlier. He wonders what he will say to Abigail to be more persuasive the second time around. His charm seems to dry up in the woman's presence, in part because of her appearance. She is a handsome woman.

Nadine allows him the use of her buckboard, so he is able to leave the boarding house just as the sun sets. The skies are overcast. Colors of pink and peach paint the cloud bottoms, cheering him for a few minutes. But when the sky darkens, he feels a knot build in his stomach. Billy's pace does not help. The buckboard moves with the slow, steady crawl of a funeral procession.

A full house at Hanson's. Hanson has a Dr. Pepper on the counter waiting as August enters, though the taste of the beverage has lost its appeal. Hanson seems relieved to see him. He smiles, touches his waxed mustache, and pats the strands of hair atop his head. "This one is free, my friend," he says.

August thanks him and turns. He recognizes the doctor who supplied him with his laudanum. There is an open chair next to him, so August sits.

The doctor looks up from his newspaper, nods, and returns to his reading. He has a glass of whiskey in front of him, but it appears untouched.

The rest of the room is filled with an assortment of railroad men and townspeople. No women—not a surprise. August knows some of the men. Russell Walters, the offensive mill owner, sits with Truthful Scully and tiny Nute Rivers. The latter wears a shirt two sizes too large. The mood of the room seems jovial, and August tries to relax.

The doctor rustles his paper and glances at August. "News from the Philippines," he says. "The Spaniards sent Fernando Primo de Rivera to serve as the new governor-general."

"I'm not familiar with the name," August says. "What is your interpretation of the news?"

"He's made a career of putting down insurrections. The Spaniards sent him to put down the current rebellion." The doctor shakes his paper. "He may succeed. But Spain's man in Cuba will not. War is the only answer."

"It's a poor question that has war for an answer," August says.

The doctor glares at him. His pupils are pinpoints. Perhaps he has been partaking in his own laudanum supply.

August sips his drink in order to give his mouth something to do besides speak.

"How is your affliction?" the doctor asks.

"Unchanged, I think. I'm grateful for the medication."

"Of course, of course," the doctor says, bobbing his head. He shakes the paper again. "I believe the airship nonsense has run its course. Tomfoolery, but the newspapers must peddle their wares, same as the rest of us." His voice carries a lilt, halfway between amusement and certitude.

"Hey." One of the railroad men calls out to August. Is he a yardman from the night before? Or is he one of the men he talked about train wrecks with the previous week? August can't tell for certain.

"You still staying at the Martin house?" he demands.

The room is suddenly quiet.

"Why, yes. I am." August manages a smile.

"You live under the same roof as that woman?"

Murmurs of laughter.

August glances at the doctor, who shrugs. August grips his Dr. Pepper bottle and then releases his hold. The doctor puts down his newspaper and clears his throat. "Delicate matter," he says.

"Yes," August agrees.

Most of the other men in the room have returned to their conversations. The man who yelled at him—the yardman—is downing his whiskey.

"There are surgical remedies for her situation, you know," the doctor says. He taps his index finger against his lips before continuing. "There is a consensus in the medical community that pelvic disorders are the chief cause of insanity among women. There are two main branches of thought in the matter. Gynecologists believe that the matter of Sapphism can be traced to lesions and other irritations in the generative track. Tell me, are you familiar with the term clitoris?"

August nods.

"An enlarged or irritated clitoris leaves its victim in a state of constant arousal." He pauses to sip his whiskey. He winces and nods. "Very good whiskey, considering the source. Where was I? Ah. The gynecologist sees only the physical aspect of the problem.

The problem with specialism is that their range of inquiry is narrowed to their own field of operation. A gynecologist sees gynecological problems. The alienist, however, recognizes a mental element as well."

August shifts in his seat and then shifts again.

"I think that in this particular case, the alienist may have a point. Sapphism is regarded as a rejection of natural roles, including motherhood. I understand that the woman in question had a child out of wedlock. Perhaps her experiences caused her to develop an unhealthy fear of men. Serial masturbation is another possibility. It is well known that compulsive masturbation causes an enlarged clitoris." The doctor senses August's discomfort. "Shall I change the subject, my friend?"

"Please continue," August says.

The doctor leans closer in order to lower his voice. "There is some outrage among our fellows, here, owing to the race of her partner in sexual commerce. For my part, I was not surprised. It's generally accepted that the congenital enlargement of the clitoris is common among certain African races." He sits back.

"You spoke of a surgical remedy." August's voice is almost too low to hear.

"A thorough examination of the clitoris can reveal any obvious lesions. In the very worst case, we will perform a clitoridectomy to restore reason to the unhappy woman."

"Restore reason?"

The doctor nods with some enthusiasm. He has an educated audience, and he seems quite full of himself. "As I said before, specialists sometimes misunderstand things, or perhaps they don't understand the context. A pastor will tell you that Sapphism is a sin. A gynecologist will tell you it's a pelvic disorder. But an alienist recognizes that an aspect of mental illness is in play." He nods again, as if agreeing with himself.

"What's intended, then?"

"We'll have the Martin woman sent to Fort Worth," the doctor says. "Halfway measures are preferred. The possible afflictions of the mind will be seriously considered." He pauses to sip his whiskey again. When he's done wincing, he continues. "If it's necessary to unsex the poor woman, the operation is largely perfected. There's a fellow in England—Baker Brown is his name. He did a large number of clitoridectomies—too many, I'm told. A clitoridectomy for epilepsy? Not prudent."

August considers his Dr. Pepper. Not the soft drink, but rather, the bottle, which would make a splendid weapon.

"The operation is fairly simple. Chloroform first. Then, snip off the clitoris with scissors. Plug the bleeding with graduated compress lint and a pad. Wrap it in a bandage, and there you are. If there's no infection, the woman will be back home with her daughter in as little as a month."

"And what of the colored woman?"

The doctor shrugs. "There are doctors of her race in Fort Worth as well. I cannot vouch for the conditions of their operating rooms, but those of African descent are hardy sorts. I would wager money on her chances."

August nods. "And when will all this happen?"

The doctor tilts his head in the direction of the others. "Up to them, I suppose. I'll be there, of course, to oversee her safety."

August pushes himself up. The yardman who'd called out to him earlier watches closely. Nute Rivers wears a sullen expression. Russell Walters, the mill owner, laughs, taps Nute on the shoulder and says, "*Martin ist eine Zungenhund.*"

August turns back to the doctor and says, "I'm staying at the boarding house. I have a two-shot derringer there. If you come for Nadine Martin, I'll be there, and I'll put one bullet in each of your eyes."

The doctor's reaction is so comical that August must suppress a laugh. The man's blue eyes water. His mouth hangs open, his lower jaw slightly askew. He tries to speak, but his tongue and lips will not deliver discernable words. He is either gagging or choking. August hobbles out of the general store, waving a hasty goodbye to Hanson, who stands wide-eyed at the counter. By the time August reaches the buckboard, his skin is tingling. He urges Billy to move, heading onto the road. He can hear calls behind him. He does not pause to look back.

The overcast sky has swallowed the starlight and the night air is electric with hints of a coming storm. He can barely see. The road is a dim ghost with more in common with shadows and smoke than with dirt and gravel. Billy seems to know where he's going, and August is grateful. August shakes in his seat, taken by both anger and fear. With the exception of the proprietor, the men in Hanson's are barbarians. The doctor, though, is something worse. Something demonic that somehow fits this dark evening.

He sees movement to his right. A thrill races through him. The deer from the boarding house, running parallel to the buckboard? He blinks, and the field is empty—the emptiness of a dark hallway or an unlit closet. He urges Billy on, tapping him with the reins and clucking. Billy begins to trot. "Good boy," August says. His voice is thin, slipping off into the night.

What must he do? Come morning, he will pay Abigail another visit. He will insist that she accompany him to the boarding house. He will send word to Ackerman to join him. Perhaps a show of numbers will convince the town that the cost involved in taking the women to Fort Worth is too great.

The buckboard crunches forward, wheels on gravel, bouncing on ruts. August does not turn around, but he listens for the sound of someone following him. His breath comes fast. His heart hammers. He should have gone to Hanson's armed. He placed too much faith in his ability to persuade. One cannot argue with barbarians or reason with demons.

August can see light from the boarding house in the distance.

Too much distance, for he can hear hoofbeats from behind.

He slaps Billy with the reins. "Gallop," he says. In the war, his horse knew one-word commands, and gallop was one of them. Billy maintains his trot. He does not understand the command. August shakes the reins again. "Faster, Billy."

He will not glance back, but he knows that the men following him are closing in. He can hear them over the blood pounding in his ears. He wheels the buckboard into the boarding house yard, but a rider on his right has already pulled past him. August yanks on the reins. The boarding house door flies open, and MacGregor, lantern in hand, steps out on the porch, armed with kitchen knife.

Laughter.

The rider on the left races past August, slapping his face as he passes, nearly knocking him from the buckboard. The other rider hefts a rock and throws it through the front window. The sound of shattering glass cuts the night into a hundred pieces.

August tries to right himself. He rubs his wet mouth with the back of his hand. The light from the porch reveals a splash of red.

MacGregor is shouting in a high-pitched voice, waving his knife. "I'll give ye a skelpit lug, ye clarty chancer!" His hair is in wild disarray, and he seems in danger of pitching off the front of the porch.

"Calm down, old man," says the rider who threw the rock.

The other rider has circled again, and as he passes August, he gives his arm a tug, spilling him from the wagon.

"We'll be back," the rider promises. With that, the two men race off into the darkness.

MacGregor hobbles down the steps and comes to August's side. August is on the ground, spitting dirt and rubbing at his mouth. MacGregor bends over with some effort and tries to hoist August to his feet. Together, they manage to put August upright. "Are they gone?" August asks.

"Aye," MacGregor says. "I think they had enough for one night."

August pants for a moment, and then says, "They're lucky they left when they did. No telling what we might have done."

"Aye. We're a fierce pair."

August puts a hand on MacGregor's shoulder. "Thank you."

MacGregor puts an arm around August and helps him toward the porch, step by painful step. August is seeing shadows everywhere, so he does not take seriously what is taking shape at the side of the house. When MacGregor stops, he realizes that he's not imagining.

Dark figures are coming from the field.

"How many?" August whispers.

"Looks like two. The knife is on the porch—"

August pulls away. "Get it," he says.

Two shapes. One large, one small. August weaves in place. His bloody mouth is throbbing now. The fall from the buckboard left him bruised. He tries to straighten up. "Hello," he calls.

No answer.

They're closer now. The large one is impossibly large. A man or a bear? MacGregor is fumbling around on the porch, looking for his knife. The shapes come closer, visible now in the glow from MacGregor's lantern.

Bose and Abigail Williams.

"Hello," August repeats.

Bose doesn't answer. Abigail steps closer. "Is Nadine here?"

"I'm here," Nadine says. She's on the porch now, dressed in her robe. "My God, Abby! What happened?"

Nadine rushes to Abigail and wraps her arms around her. Abigail melts into her shoulder, sobbing. "They came to my house," she says. "They broke all my things and threw them in the yard." Her voice is hard to understand because she is crying so hard. "Bose came and got me just before they arrived. If he'd been even a minute later—"

Nadine stands like a statue. "Did they see you leaving?"

"No," Bose answers.

"You will stay here," Nadine says.

"My things . . . all gone," Abigail wails.

"Just things," Nadine says.

"My books," she says. "They stood outside, tearing the pages."

Nadine looks to Bose. "You'll stay here tonight. I've two empty rooms upstairs."

MacGregor frowns.

"I'll sleep outside, if I sleep," Bose says. His face is like a sheet of Texas limestone. August notices that the man has a pistol—an old Colt—tucked in his pants. Good.

Nadine and Abigail move toward the house. August looks ahead and sees Natalie on the porch, rubbing her neck. The lantern lights her young face. Her eyes are wide, and her mouth twitches.

Bose is already walking off into the field. MacGregor moves toward the porch. August follows slowly, feeling each of his eighty-six years. Another glance at Natalie tells him she's crying. As he reaches the bottom porch step, he hears her whisper, "My fault."

He waits until he's at the top step to say, "Help me, child. I can't carry that lantern." He pauses to catch her eye. "Natalie? You didn't know."

"I said—"

"You didn't know," he repeats, putting a hand on her shoulder. "Now, you know. You made a mistake. What you do next is the only thing that's important."

CHAPTER TWENTY-ONE

Martins' Boarding House
Wednesday, April 28, 1897

When August wakes, he finds he can barely move. The pain comes from his knees, his shoulders, and his hip. He grits his teeth and struggles free of the blankets. Tumbling from the wagon the night before has hobbled him. The effort required to rise is extraordinary, for the bedding is as persistent as any set of shackles. No matter. There is medicine in the dresser just six feet away, and he will do most anything to get to it.

By the time he is dressed and moving with some surety, breakfast is over. Nadine kept a biscuit for him, wrapped in a napkin, and he is grateful. He is nearly shaking with hunger. Three bites into the biscuit, he is full.

Outside, MacGregor is tending to Billy. When August arrives, the old Scot does not hesitate. "Did ye know?"

August shrugs. He assumes MacGregor is talking about Nadine and Abigail. "She told me Monday morning. When did she tell you?"

"Yesterday. And what do ye think?"

MacGregor has hitched Billy to the buckboard. August busies himself checking the harness.

"She's poking a tink."

August turns so quickly, he strains his neck. "Shame on you!" he barks.

MacGregor folds his arms and scowls.

August returns his gaze to Billy. He can feel his face burn. He's made a bad start. He hopes to go into town to shore up some support for Nadine. If he cannot do that here at home, among friends, he will not fare well with the people of Rhome. MacGregor has turned to go. "Wait, please."

MacGregor turns back.

"I am sorry for snapping, my friend. Let me explain. I've a dog in this hunt. Nadine has been family since she was a teen."

"Aye. Ye said as much."

"When you say *tink*, you mean something dirty. That woman is as far from dirt as Margaret of Wessex."

MacGregor flinches as if he's been slapped.

"I understand your feelings, and I share some of them. Men were meant to be with women, and women were meant to be with men. But what happens when the doors are closed is not our concern. We are *Americans.* We live our lives, answering to no one but Providence."

"They're hell bound."

"No one who lives should be measured with a single yardstick." August waves his hands for emphasis. "Nadine is as good a woman as any in Texas. You know this is true. She's waited on you since the day you entered the boarding house."

"Aye, right." Sarcasm.

"Tell the truth, MacGregor. Is the food she serves better than any other boarding house you've lived in?"

He starts to disagree but stops himself. MacGregor is an honest man.

"She never sits with us. She *waits* on us." August says.

"She has no servants—"

"Do you think she'd suddenly become royalty if she did?"

"No."

"Do you ever miss a meal? Does she save food for you?"

"Yes, but I hear about it. She has a thousand rules."

"And she enforces *none* of them when your comfort is at stake."

MacGregor frowns. His wrinkles form patterns on his face. "But she's . . . prickly."

"That she is," August says. "I wouldn't argue the point. But there's more involved. Let me tell you what they do to women like Nadine and Abigail." He recounts the doctor's explanation, from scissors to sutures.

MacGregor shoves his hands in his pockets and toes the grass. "Crivvens," he mutters.

Billy snorts. August climbs onto the buckboard. "The people in town don't know Nadine. We do. This cannot happen. If worst comes to worst, I hope you'll stand with us."

MacGregor shakes his head. "I dinnae like the Williams girl's brother. That uppity cowboy."

August laughs. "There isn't a Brit alive who wouldn't say the same thing about a Scot."

MacGregor laughs before he can stop himself. "Ye might be too cliver for me."

"Keeping up with a Scot takes agility."

MacGregor nods. "All right, I'm with ye." He pauses. "With reservations."

. . .

August's first stop is Hanson's. The mercantile's namesake is tending an empty house, so August has a chance to talk.

"A Dr. Pepper?" Hanson asks.

"No," August says. "Too early in the day. But I wanted to talk to you."

He gives August a solemn nod.

"Last night. Very disturbing—"

"It was," Hanson said. "Actually, I'm glad you're here. I need to warn you. They're planning to visit the boarding house tonight."

"No."

"Yes," Hanson says, sadness etching his face. "Nadine Martin has been a good customer for years. I will be sorry to lose her."

"You won't lose her," August says. "Tell me, who is coming?"

"Well, the railroad has been no friend to the Martins. They want revenge, though I'm not sure what they want revenge for. And that Kraut who runs the flour mill says he's bringing his employees. Nute Rivers is with them. The pastor—"

"Not everyone feels the same as those," August says. He sounds as if he's voicing a question.

Hanson purses his lips. "I don't, for one. As I said, Nadine's been a good neighbor. She buys her supplies from me, pays me on time, and doesn't complain if the meat has a bit of sawdust on it."

August smiles. "That is a good neighbor indeed."

"Something to appreciate," Hanson says, pulling at his mustache.

The next stop is the livery stable. Royce Jenkins and his son are there. "You were very kind to Bill Ackerman as regards his horse," he says. Then August asks if they've heard about the problem the railroad men have with Nadine.

"Sure did," Royce says. His son—a thin, reedy sort with uncombed hair and pimples—nods as well.

"You're good to your animals. I suspect that you're predisposed to kindness in general."

Royce Jenkins narrows his gaze.

"There's a rumor that some railroad boys, and maybe some people in town, will be coming out to the boarding house to take Nadine Martin away. You wouldn't be planning to join them, would you?"

Jenkins stares a hole through August. His expression is flat as an East Texas field. "I make up my own mind, and it's none of your business." He spits. "But I'll tell you this. Those railroad boys stay here because they aren't welcome at the Martin boarding house. They're *my* problem now. They get drunk, shit and piss in my loft, and part with their money like sheenies. We've got no love for those bastards."

August exhales as if he's been holding his breath.

"As for Nadine Martin, I don't give a damn if she sleeps with horses."

Royce's son laughs. "Just not our horses."

Royce cuffs the boy.

. . .

His next visit is unsatisfactory. The town's doctor is in no mood for a reconciliation. "Find your medicine elsewhere," he shouts, which does not surprise August. The man cannot stand to be challenged in his beliefs. That a man of the medical sciences cannot bear the examination of his proclamations is a disgrace.

For a space of three seconds, August considers visiting the mill owner, but he has no time to waste on a cretin.

He encounters a few people on the road. If he knows them, he engages them in conversation. Most have not heard of Nadine's troubles, nor do they seem interested. They have troubles of their own.

He recognizes the town blacksmith. Ned Heath is a stout man, perhaps in his thirties, with forearms like hog shanks. August sits atop the buckboard, too tired to climb down and shake the man's massive hands.

Heath pulls at his beard, prematurely gray, and interrupts August halfway through his speech. "Got no time for railroad boys," he says. "They don't pay their invoices on time. Only sure way to get paid is to delay a repair until they decide they can't do without me, which isn't often. They don't like the Martin woman? That's enough for me. I'm siding with her."

"The situation is complex—"

"No, it ain't. Those railroad boys can go to blazes."

Fatigued, August turns home. If he makes good time, he will arrive at the boarding house in time to wash up and attend supper, something he has not done on a consistent basis.

Along the way, August scans the landscape. The doe he's become attached to is nowhere in sight. Why would it be? Anyone with a musket or rifle could shoot the beast and put the meat aside. The fact that the doe appears to him unharmed is a miracle. He remembers his intent for coming to Rhome—*I want to see a miracle.* He shakes his head. Venison is not the miracle he needs.

Back at the boarding house, MacGregor joins him to help unhook Billy from his burden. He's silent at first. "Ye shamed me."

August puts a hand on his shoulder. "We're friends."

MacGregor nods. "Aye." He has a plug of tobacco in his cheek, and he spits. "Is a storm coming?"

August nods. "Tonight."

.   .   .

There is little conversation at supper. Natalie is hiding in her bedroom. Nadine delivers a serving plate for the men at the table and heads out to the porch, where she dines with Abigail and Bose. August feels a gnawing irritation at separate dining locations, but the others probably don't share his modern opinions. Would it be so awful for Bose and Abigail to share the kitchen table?

First things first. He needs to ask Chambers to stand with him. One inequity at a time.

At the end of the war, August ate with his men. Five hundred meals? Beans. Hardtack. Nothing like the spread Nadine has put out—soused pork, cornbread, stewed fruit and a pitcher of tea—the kind of meal a soldier in the field dreams of. Looking around the table, August wishes that a few of his old comrades were here with him tonight. Grizzled old Samuel with his hand-carved pipe. Corporal Washington and his bad teeth. Fighting men.

"Gentlemen," August said. "I need to inform you of something."

MacGregor studies his empty supper plate. He knows what's coming. He'd promised to stand with August, but he might have changed his mind.

"Rumor has it that we'll be visited tonight by vigilantes. They are coming for Nadine and Abigail. From here, the women will be taken to Fort Worth. There, a doctor will remove their private parts, believing that to be a cure for love and friendship." MacGregor slumps down in his chair, his gaze still on the plate. Chambers sits with his mouth open.

"I intend to stand on the porch and greet them. I have a two-shot derringer in my travel case. If the matter comes to violence, there will be at least two men dead." He is careful not to sound boastful. His calm demeanor may encourage them.

"You want our help defending the house," Chambers says. His few strands of hair spill over his forehead.

"How do ye intend to defend this castle?" MacGregor says. "Too many windows."

"Agreed," August says.

"What do you want us to do?" Chambers looks frightened.

"I think our best chance to avoid violence is to present a united front. If we see them coming—"

"If?" MacGregor asks.

"If we see them coming, I intend to greet them from the porch. If there are enough of us there, they'll stand down."

MacGregor grins. "A fine plan. Stand there like targets?"

"You agree then?"

Chambers pushes back from the table and raises his cane. "I don't have a weapon, other than this cane. But if someone tries to grab Miss Nadine, I'll lay open a cheek or two with tip."

MacGregor turns. "So, ye intend to stand with him?"

Chambers nods, his chest puffed out.

MacGregor turns back to August. "Well, then. You have a company to command, General Simms." He winks. "They're already afeart of my knife hand, as you learned last evening."

August smiles. "Thank you," he says.

"Now, we're three old fools. Not just two." He tilts his head in the direction of the porch. "Will the big man be joining us? I see he's packing a hogleg."

August stands. He is tired, and his legs feel weak. "Let's find out."

Bose is on the far side of the porch, sitting in the chair August thinks of as his. Abigail sits next to him. Nadine is standing, her supper plate on the porch rail. She looks up as August approaches. He stops short, standing with his hands folded in front. MacGregor and Chambers stand behind him.

"When I went to town," he begins, "Hanson told me some of the townsfolk and some railroad men would be coming here tonight to take Nadine and Abigail. We intend to greet them at the porch and turn them away."

Bose glares at them for a few moments, shakes his head, and turns to Abigail. "This place ain't safe. Grab your things. We gone."

CHAPTER TWENTY-TWO

Martins' Boarding House
Wednesday, April 28, 1897

Bose Williams stands, supper plate in hand. He glances down at his sister Abigail, who is still seated. "Come on," he orders. "We leave now, we'll be on the road before anybody knows we gone."

August unfolds his hands. "Our chances are better if we stand together." He gestures to MacGregor and Chambers. "These fine men will stand with us."

Bose doesn't laugh, not exactly. August suspects that the cowboy's stony face won't allow it. But there's a sardonic turn of the lip to his expression now, echoed in his words. "Three old men going to stop a lynch mob? A little breeze blow you aside." He glances back at Abigail, who hasn't moved. "Come on."

"Who do you think you're speaking to?" Abigail asks.

"I'm talking to you," Bose says. "We're leaving now. This ain't up for discussion."

"And what about Nadine?" Abigail asks.

Bose waves his hand in August's direction. "She got these *fine men* to protect her."

Abigail glowers, her amber eyes catching the reflection of a setting sun. Her lips are pursed in anger. "I don't blame you. Go. But I'm staying here. And you are right. This is not up for discussion."

The soft buzz of katydids underscores her words. The men and women regard each other. A tiny breeze crosses the field, ruffling the saw grass. August clears his throat. "I have a derringer. Yours won't be the only gun."

"How much ammunition do you have?" Bose asks, scowling.

"Two shots. That's all." August points at Bose's pistol. "You have extra ammunition for your Colt?"

Bose shakes his head.

"Well, that's six shots—"

"Five," Bose says. "I keep the hammer on an empty chamber."

August nods. "Normally, I'd call that good sense."

Bose coughs, perhaps to stifle the long-awaited laugh.

"I have a shotgun," Nadine says. "I keep it loaded in the bedroom." The men gaze at her in surprise. "In case one of you gets out of line," she explains.

"How many shells?" August asks.

"Just the two. Two barrels. Two shells."

August seems to relax, hands on his hips. "Well, then. We're fine. Unless more than nine folks show up."

Nervous laughter, but laughter just the same.

"I think we should avoid the usual convention of a warning shot," August adds.

Bose sticks out his lower jaw. "I'll fire a warning shot into the first sumbitch that makes a move to the porch."

August nods. "Good plan. But let me talk to them first."

"Ain't no words gonna stop a crowd that wants blood. I seen it, and you know I seen it."

"Just the same," August says. "Let me talk."

"You plan to just stand out here and greet them?"

August gestures at the house. "This place is too big. Can't defend it."

Bose turns to his sister. "You hear the man? Can't defend this place. And you want to stay here and wait for a crowd of white men to take you like they took our daddy?"

"I'm staying with Nadine." Abigail's voice is as cool as the evening breeze.

"Bose," August says. "If they see us lined up, three of us armed, they'll lose their nerve." He turns to MacGregor. "You can handle a shotgun, can't you?"

"He'll have to get his own," Nadine says. "They're coming for me. I'll keep my shotgun, thank you." MacGregor shakes his head, a wry smile on his face.

August notices that Natalie is standing at the corner of the house. It's not clear how long she's been listening.

"I don't know if they'll really come for us tonight," August says. "Rumors like that can be as useless as a newspaper article." Then, trying for levity, he adds, "Or so I've heard."

No one laughs.

"What is your plan, exactly?" Bose asks.

August tries to sound confident. "There are six of us here. We stand out front, weapons in hand but not pointed, and I talk sense into them."

"Seven," Natalie says, stepping closer to the others. "There are seven of us."

"You will be in your bedroom, young lady—"

"No, I will not," Natalie says. Her voice is calm and determined—the voice of a young woman. "I will be standing next to you."

Bose shakes his head. "Too many women with too many opinions round here."

August looks up the road. The soft breeze and thrum of insects is soothing. How could there be trouble in a world so serene? A thought comes unbidden, and it sends a shiver down his back. The night might amount to nothing at all—or it might be the last night of his life.

When he was young, he knew that death would eventually come, but he lived the life of an adventurer, as if he were immortal. When his mother and father passed, mortality had a bit more meaning, as always happens when parents die. The war brought home the capricious nature of death. At Chaffin's Farm, a man on either side of him fell in battle. He'd escaped with a superficial wound—a bullet creased his bicep. It bled plenty, but he healed. It wasn't until his wife died that he began to regard his remaining life as a ticking clock. Would the ticking stop tonight?

"Here's my thought," August says. "If we stay inside, and try to defend an attack, then we've already lost." He turns to Bose. "You ever see the elephant?"

"What the hell are you talking about?"

"War. Have you ever fired that gun in battle?"

"No," Bose admits. "I cowboy for a living. I ain't no soldier."

"I was a soldier," August says. "And I'm telling you—the best way to avoid blood being spilled tonight is to stand out here and greet whatever comes our way, head on. If we hide inside and a shot is fired, they'll burn this place to the ground with us in it."

Bose doesn't speak.

"Your thoughts? You disagree?" August prompts.

The question seems to startle Bose. He thinks for a moment, and then says, "None of this is up to me. Y'all are calling the shots here. Three women and an old man." He points at MacGregor and Chambers. "You two fools are in my world, now."

Chambers lifts his cane and puffs out his chest. "I have this."

The moment is so absurd that even Bose has to laugh, though he tries to cover it with a fist and another coughing fit.

When the noise settles, August says, "Nadine? Abigail? This involves you most directly. Do you have anything you want to add?"

Nadine shakes her head.

Abigail looks to Bose, and when she catches his eye, she whispers, "Thank you."

"Don't thank me," he says. "Y'all are crazy."

.   .   .

It's full dark outside, so they sit around the kitchen table. Nadine has the lantern lit. MacGregor is out behind the house in case someone comes from the blind side of the house. Chambers is sitting on the front porch, his cane in his lap, scanning the road.

"They may wait until they think we're asleep," Nadine says.

"They may not come at all," Abigail says.

"I don't sleep much." August shifts in his chair, trying to relieve the pain in his back. He does not want to take a night dose of his medicine. He needs his mind at the ready. "I will sit on the porch later tonight." He turns to Bose. "You can sleep in my room, if you like."

Bose squints as if August has asked him to fly. "No. I'll stay out back. I'll wake you all up when those cowards come creeping."

"They're coming to *collect* us," Nadine says. "They think they're performing a service. They'll walk right up the road, like they're delivering feed. August is right."

August reaches into his pocket, touching the handle of his derringer.

"So, let me ask a question," Abigail says. "What happens if people come here, and they don't listen to August? What if they try to push past and grab us?"

"I'll put a hole in a few o' them boys, that's what." Bose sits back, checking the loads in his Colt.

Abigail seems near tears. "If people start shooting, you'll end up dead, Bose. I couldn't stand that. And you wouldn't be the only one."

"Am I supposed to let them take you?" Bose's lips pull back, and he crinkles his nose.

"I don't want people to die," Abigail says.

"Then what are we bothering with guns for?" Bose demands. "Just for show?" He gives an exasperated sigh. "We should have left here hours ago."

August says, "Whether or not people die is in their hands. Their choice."

"I don't know," Abigail says. "I just don't want—"

"We can't argue about this now," Nadine says.

August puts both hands on the table, palms down. "Better now than later when they're here. Let's decide what we're going to do and then do it."

"They might not come," Natalie says. "Abby said so."

Abigail glances at Natalie and gives her a sad smile. This is the first time Natalie has acknowledged her presence since coming to the boarding house the night before. Natalie smiles back. It's a beautiful smile.

"Here is the central question. Are we going to allow them to take Nadine and Abigail? If not, then either we pack up and run, or we accept the fact that we may have to fight."

"I'm not leaving my home," Nadine says.

The house is silent then. The lantern flickers, sending shadows dancing off into the corners of the room. Outside, the night is still black. Later, a waning sliver of moon will rise, but the clouds may swallow it up. August licks his lips. His mouth is dry as a Texas creek bed. "We stay, then. Abigail, I admire your resistance to violence. I truly do. But you intend to stay here, and Nadine intends to stay here. That means we may have to fight." He catches a glimpse of Natalie's face. The girl is terrified. "I don't think it will come to that, though."

More silence. Waiting fills the space between their fear and the coming storm. The slow, agonizing progression from second to second is filled with regrets and thoughts of what might still go wrong. August whispers an apology to whatever God might be listening—something he's done before every battle he's ever fought. One thing is certain. When they go to stand on the porch, he will stand just to the right of Bose, so he can reach over and grab the man's gun hand. He does not want Bose to fire before giving August a chance to talk.

After a while, Bose dozes off sitting up. His head cocked back, he snores and wakes himself up. Abigail touches his arm. "You might go lay down for a while."

"I'm fine, I'm fine."

They all jump when Mr. Chambers comes through the door. "They're coming," he says.

Everyone stands. August touches a finger to his lips—a kiss for a wife who is no longer here. "Natalie?" he says. "Would you go to the back and fetch Mr. MacGregor for us?"

Natalie scurries off. Bose stands and coughs to clear his throat. His eyes have a shine to them that worries August. Abigail is trembling. Only Nadine seems calm. She retrieves her shotgun from the counter, checks the loads, grabs the lantern and heads for the door.

The people coming are carrying torches. They are still some distance away, but they will arrive in minutes.

August stands in front of the porch steps. "You stand here with me," he tells Bose.

The cowboy frowns and says, "Yes, Cap'n." He takes his place on August's left. Abigail stands at Bose's other arm.

Nadine walks into the yard and sets the lantern on the ground. As she returns to the porch, she pulls back the hammers on the double-barrel shotgun, keeping it pointed up. Chambers stands to her right. When Natalie returns, she wedges between Nadine and Chambers.

MacGregor is the last to join them, holding the knife he'd held the night before. He stands on the far left, next to Abigail.

The crowd bearing torches is perhaps a hundred yards away. "My eyes are bad," August says. "Anybody carrying a gun?"

Bose squints into the dark. "Yep. Looks like a rifle or two. Maybe more." He frowns. "There's another crowd coming behind them." He puts his hand on his pistol.

August clutches Bose's forearm. "Not yet," he says.

The first group arrives. Flickering torches throw a single shadow that stretches across the yard like a leviathan reaching for the porch. No one speaks. The pounding blood at his temples is all August can hear.

When they stop, ten yards shy of the porch, August clears his throat. "Howdy," he calls. "Pretty late for a visit."

CHAPTER TWENTY-THREE

Martins' Boarding House
Tuesday, April 27, 1897

Truthful Scully steps forward, a grin on his face. He wipes his brow with his cap and points at the porch. "Came here to help this woman." He glances at Abigail and waves the cap. "That one, too." All the while, one eye is locked on Bose. "I see you got meat in the pot."

Bose taps his holster. "Sure do."

"Well, you'd have to be some kind of stupid to shoot a white man." He's still grinning, but his face is wet with sweat.

"Where's your friends from the mill? And the doctor?" August asks.

Scully shrugs. "Doctor was reluctant to join us. Says you threatened him." Another man taps Scully's shoulder and hooks a thumb behind him. More torches approaching. "That might be them now," Scully says. His smile broadens. "Me and the boys are on an errand of mercy, so to speak. Didn't come to court trouble."

"Came armed, though," Bose says. Two of the six men carry hunting rifles. Another one has a crowbar over his shoulder.

Scully shakes his head. "Now, considering our intentions and all, that was downright rude of you." He points his cap again, this time at Natalie. "There's bystanders here. Hate to have someone take a bullet because a few old men and an uppity—"

"More than one of us is armed," Nadine says.

Smile gone, Scully takes another step toward the porch. "You're a cattish sort of woman. You need to put that piece down and come on out here." His cockeyed gaze serves him now, for he's able to keep one eye on Bose while he talks to Nadine. "Come on. What you're doing is a sin in the eyes of God."

Marching feet announce the arrival of the second group. One man stands at the forefront. He's a thin sort, wearing old shoes and coveralls. He lifts a hand, waving at the people on the porch.

Bill Ackerman.

"Howdy to you, August," he says.

"Hello, Bill. What brings you out this late?"

Ackerman laughs. "Heard some railroad boys might come around tonight. We thought we'd show up, just in case. Let those boys know that we don't like vigilantes." He frowns at the six railroad employees. "We heard they tore up Miss Abigail's house. Figured we'd dissuade them from a similar crime." After a pause, he continues. This time, his voice is loud enough for everyone behind him to hear. "They needed to know we're a community here. We mind our own business—unless some fool tries to harm one of us. Then, there's the devil to pay." The crowd murmurs its approval.

Scully glances to his coworkers for reassurance, but they are backing away. His smile returns, but he's twisting the cap in his hands like he wants to choke it. "Well then," he says. "I guess y'all don't want our help." Alone now, he surveys the crowd, then squares his shoulders, nods at Ackerman, and turns to leave.

Bose takes a step toward the porch stairs, but August blocks his way.

The crowd watches as the six railroad employees slip off into the darkness. Ackerman turns back to the people on the porch. "Miss Abigail? Tell your brother not to shoot. We're friendly."

Nervous laughter.

Nadine's cool demeanor is gone now. She lowers the hammers on her shotgun and sets the gun against the chair behind her. Her hands are shaking.

August walks into the yard. He holds out a hand, but Ackerman pulls him in for a hug, slapping his back.

To August's left, another man steps into the lantern's light, hat in hand. Pastor Allen. "Nadine?" he calls. She is hard to see, hidden in shadow.

"Yes, Pastor," she says. She sounds startled.

"Proverbs 6: 16 to 19 tells us the things the Lord hates. *Haughty eyes, a lying tongue, hands that shed innocent blood, a heart that devises wicked plans, feet that make haste to run to evil, a false witness who breathes out lies, and one who sows discord among brothers.* You are *none* of those things. A friend—" He stops to glance at August. "A friend reminded me of your virtues, and they are plentiful. As for sin, John 13 tells us . . ." His voice trails off, followed by an uncomfortable silence. Finally, he clears his throat. "Well, at least you're not a Presbyterian."

The crowd, Methodists all, erupts in laughter and eases closer to the house. Pastor Allen, hat still in hand, walks to the porch where Nadine is standing. He reaches up. Nadine bends over the rail, taking his hand.

Abigail calls to someone at the back of the crowd. Two colored men, a father and son, move to the porch rail. They are her neighbors, and she greets them like family.

As the townspeople mill around the front steps, Natalie comes from the house, a tray of water glasses in hand. Nadine cocks her head as if to ask a question. Natalie says, "Walking all the way out here at night is thirsty business." She carries the tray down the steps and begins serving guests as if the yard were a ballroom. August stares, open-mouthed. Is this the same pouty little girl he thought he knew?

Nadine comes down a moment later, holding a second lantern. The light casts a sepia glow across the yard, adding to the flickering orange of torches. Men stand in small groups, smiling and laughing. The night air carries a parade of spring rain smells—damp saw grass, dandelions, and black gumbo clay soil. The rising moon is hidden, but its glow backlights the clouds.

Ned Heath, the blacksmith, shares a flask with two other men. One lights a cigar and blows smoke into the night air. Natalie returns with another tray of beverages—tea this time. The teenaged son of one of the men from town follows her like a puppy with an urge to heel.

August feels a sudden draining sensation. The tensions of the evening have sapped his reserves. He moves to the porch, where he finds Bose sitting down, a blank expression on his face. His mustache is twisted on the left, as if he's been pulling at it absently. August smiles when he reaches the top step.

"Doesn't make up for it," Bose says. His voice is gravel.

"If you mean your father," August says, shrugging, "how could it?"

Bose looks away, his expression still blank. His eyes are a different matter.

August leans against the porch railing for support. "Still and all, these folks came out to help us. That's something."

Bose scowls. "They were here for Nadine. Didn't have nothing to do with Abby or me."

"Well, Nadine and Abby are a couple. You should get used to it. I have. Help one and you're helping the other."

Bose nods in the direction of the men in the yard. Ned Heath is making fast work of his flask. "You see that slab of corned beef there? I meet him on the road tomorrow, and I best stand out of his way until he passes."

August nods. "I won't deny it. But these people had a choice tonight, and they left their homes to come here. It's different from what happened fifteen years ago. By the time another fifteen years go by, bigotry might be a thing of the past."

Bose locks a fiery gaze on August. "You *believe* that?"

August doesn't flinch. "No, I guess not." He gestures toward the people in the yard. "But I'm going to act like I do for one night." Dizzy, he closes his eyes for a moment until he can get his bearings. "You know how the word bigot came about? It was an old French word. An insult to belittle the Normans. Do you see what I'm saying? The first person to use the word bigot was . . . a bigot."

"What is that supposed to mean?"

"It means that some battles are as old as mankind, and every generation is doomed to fight them." He pauses. "But not tonight."

"Why is that?"

"Because tonight, we nudged things in the right direction. We sleep deep tonight. Tomorrow, we take up the battle again."

"We nudged things, huh? Here in Rhome, Texas. Glory be."

"Yes, here in Texas. Not Boston. Not Chicago. Rhome."

Bose doesn't answer, but his head gives a tiny shake, side to side.

"How bad did they tear up Abigail's house?"

Bose slumps in his chair. "I'm sure it's bad. Watched them trashing things from a distance. Didn't stick around to see more."

"Well, she ought to stay here. Never be a better time for the town to get used to the idea."

"That part ain't right either—"

"Don't be a bigot," August says. His voice is soft and only chides a little.

Bose shakes his head, more vehemently this time. "You're a crazy old man."

Steps behind him announce Ackerman's approach. "August? How are you doing?"

"I'm tired, I guess." August rests his back against the porch support beam.

"I spoke to Nadine," he says. "I'm going to stay here tonight, just in case." He looks to Bose. "I'll keep watch. But I'm betting those railroad boys are heading out of town as we speak."

"What about the mill foreman? Walters?" August asks.

"I don't know. I'll figure that out tomorrow." Again, he turns to Bose. "Thank you for standing up with my friends," he says.

Bose doesn't answer.

"How'd you get all these people to come here?" August asks. "You did this, did you not?"

"Hell, you talked to half of these people this morning yourself. Most of the work was already done. All I had to do was act like you."

"How's that?"

"Old and crazy?" Bose asks.

August laughs, surprised. "I believe our friend Bose just told a joke."

Ackerman grins. "And he's pretty much right at that."

August looks out into the yard. Abigail and Nadine are talking to Pastor Allen and two other men, sipping glasses of tea like the evening after a barn-raising. As if the world wasn't what it surely is.

Across the yard, Natalie stands, arms folded, listening to the young man who's been following her. The boy flaps his arms and laughs. Whatever story he's telling, there's plenty of action.

A shout catches everyone's attention. Ned Heath shoves the man with the cigar, then wraps one meaty forearm around him in a headlock. Ackerman rushes into the yard. "Ned! Ned! What are you doing?" He tries to separate the men, but Ned won't let go. "Stop it! You did a good thing here, tonight. Don't ruin it!" Slowly, Ned uncoils his arm, a scowl on his face. The man he'd been holding pushes off to get away, a trickle of blood running from his nose.

August looks back at Bose. The cowboy's expression is blank again. A rockface without a fingerhold.

The next wave of dizziness leaves August swaying in place, hand to the porch support beam. "I find that I'm very tired," he mumbles.

"Not surprised," Bose says. He stands. "Let me help you inside."

"I'm fine."

"I don't think so." Bose takes his elbow.

"August?" Hanson calls from the bottom of the porch steps. His mustache looks magnificent—waxed and shaped. He holds a bottle of Dr. Pepper in his hand. "I brought this for you, sir." He holds out the bottle.

Bose steps around August and reaches out. "Thank you, Mr. Hanson."

"Thank you, Bose," Hanson says. "Nice to see you."

Bose walks August into the boarding house. Crossing the kitchen, August's legs buckle, but Bose keeps him upright with one arm, the other hand wrapped around the Dr. Pepper bottle.

When they reach the bedroom, Bose deposits August on the foot of the bed. "You need help with your clothes?" he asks.

"I'm fine, thank you."

Bose holds out the bottle. "You want this open?"

August shakes his head. "I think I'll save it. Would you put it on the dresser for me?"

Bose does so, and then turns to leave. He pauses at the door. "I strike you as ungrateful?"

"Not at all." August's shoulders slump. He looks down at his shoes. They seem very far away. "You strike me as realistic."

"Well," Bose says, his voice soft as rain, "I do appreciate you."

As the door closes, August thinks of Judge Proctor. *I appreciate you being here, just the same.* The curse of an old man's memory— the connections come unbidden. His life strikes him as a progression of noble failures in the service of justice. He might as well have tried to hold back the moon, for all the good he's done. The world resists change.

He turns to the window. The sound of people on the lawn has become indistinct, like the hum of insects. He bends over to untie his shoes, but he is dizzy, nearly spilling onto the floor. Instead, he lays back on the bed, inching toward the headboard, his shoes on top the bedding. Nadine will forgive him this, he thinks. *I've never been so tired.* But is that so? He remembers climbing down Mount Ararat after the earthquake. He remembers the last month of the war when lack of sleep and too much death left him shaking and awake for two days. He has been tired before.

This is different. He thinks of the submersible and the terrible captain that scuttled his own craft. He thinks of an airship, blown to pieces over a friend's windlass. "I am dredging memories for a metaphor," he whispers. "Finding none." He shakes his head and closes his eyes. He feels the yawning abyss, and for once, he welcomes it.

CHAPTER TWENTY-FOUR

Martin's Boarding House
Wednesday, May 12, 1897

August sits on the porch. Although the sun is out, he shivers. He is as thin as bird bones because eating has become a chore. The tastes and smells no longer appeal to him. Nadine arrives with a glass of sweet tea and a blanket. He is grateful for both—his mouth is perpetually dry.

Nadine fusses the blanket into place, tucking the corners into the chair. "Better?" she asks.

"Perfect," he says.

She crosses over and sits in the chair next to him. "I saw the solicitor, as you suggested."

"And?"

"We signed the papers yesterday. Abby owns half of this place now." She laughs softly. "Half of nothing is nothing."

"It's not nothing. It's a business going through a rough patch."

She nods. "Yes. And if something happens to either one of us, the boarding house will go on."

August gives an absent nod. "Marriage is not a possibility for you two. But you can mimic the legalities." He thinks of Judge Proctor and his marriage under false names. Would a union between Nadine and Abby be such a terrible threat to the institution? No.

"I'm sure we'll be fine," Nadine says.

August smiles to himself. She will indeed be fine, though she doesn't know how fine just yet. The money he's left her will solve many of her problems.

"How does this all work out for Natalie?"

Nadine laughs. "That girl. She wants nothing to do with the house. She wants to go to college. This airship business has infected her. She wants to be a *scientist*." She shakes her head. "As if we had the money for that."

August nods and tries not to grin. "What about Abigail's house?"

"Shambles," Nadine says. "But she's got a neighbor—one of the men who came out to protect her that night. He's done some carpentry and he wants to fix the place up. He and his son. His own place is a tarpaper shack, so he doesn't mind the damage." Her back is straight as a rail, hands in her lap. "Haven't had the usual travel trade this summer," she says. "I think the railroad folks are putting out a bad word about me."

"That won't last," August says. "You run a good house. How are things working out with Abigail?"

Nadine's expression softens. "I spent so much worry over people finding out about us. It's strange not to worry. And having her here every day is like a dream. It's like stepping through a door into a different world. It's scary and beautiful. I don't know how to explain it."

"You just did."

Nadine sighs. "Abby wants to make some changes, of course. Turns out she has a lot of ideas."

"Good ones?"

"I expect they are. Abby is smart." She frowns. "She wants me to reach out to the railroad and act like nothing's ever happened."

August takes a sip of the sweet tea and swishes it around his mouth before swallowing. "The men who wronged you are long gone."

"You have a short memory. Railroad men were coming to take Abby and me away just two weeks ago."

"I haven't forgotten," August says. He sniffs. "I was speaking of—"

"Corn Norris. I know. And the other one. Natalie's father."

In the daylight, the motte of trees on the horizon seems miles away. A breeze tousles the saw grass. He thinks of the doe. Had he really seen her? The kind of man who spends the last month of his life chasing airships might not be the best judge of reality. He closes his eyes and takes a deep breath.

Nadine wakes him when she stands. "You dozed off," she explains.

"I seem to have an easy time of that. Except at night."

Nadine bends down and takes his hand. A perfect tear rolls down her cheek. "Abby is here now, and we'll get by. My daughter seems to have grown up all at once. My life is suddenly better." She wipes the tear from her cheek. "I'm sorry we didn't get along so well at first. And I wish things didn't have to be so sad now." She shakes her head. "I will miss you."

August clears his throat. "I will miss you, too."

Nadine sniffles. More tears.

"Nadine, every true story is a sad one," he says finally, placing his hand on hers. "That's because if a story is true, it ends in death." He smiles. "It's my turn."

. . .

When the noon meal is served, Abigail delivers a tray with some tea and a piece of toast with jelly. She is wearing the clothes she cleans rooms in, but her back is straight, and her shoulders are erect. She sets the tray down next to his chair and turns to go.

"Abigail, I would request a favor from you."

"Of course," she says.

"I understand that the men who visited your house destroyed your books."

Abigail's expression clouds as she nods.

"In my room, I have five books that are important to me. One of them is a collection of Mr. Shakespeare's plays. I understand you are fond of the Bard. At any rate, I would appreciate it if you kept the books for yourself after I am gone."

"Very kind, sir."

"Great books demand to be read."

Abigail smiles. "I promise you that I will read every one of them." Pausing for a moment, she says, "Mr. Simms, may I ask you a question?"

"Of course."

She stands in front of him, her hands folded in front. "Do you not like me sir?"

The question surprises him. "I like you just fine."

The answer doesn't seem to satisfy. "I only ask because you seem so reserved around me. You're a talkative man with the others, but don't have much to say to me."

August nods. "I understand why you'd think that."

"Is it something I've done wrong?"

August coughs. "You must forgive me. I find that even at my age, I become tongue-tied in the presence of a beautiful woman."

Abigail tilts her head as if to wonder if he is making fun of her, but he is not. She blushes and then smiles. "Why you rascally old charmer." She laughs, shakes her head, and leaves him to his toast and jelly.

. . .

Ackerman comes by in the afternoon. His lazy grin reminds August of long, hot days like this one. August still has the blanket across his lap. "What brings you out here, Bill?"

"Brought you a paper," Ackerman says. He's carrying the news and a brown paper bag. "Thought you'd be interested. Says the airship mystery is solved." He unfolds the paper and hands it over. "They say it's time to put the hoax to rest."

August skims the third-page article. When he finishes, he refolds the paper.

"What do you think?"

August laughs. "I don't think the news is the last word."

"You figure the real airship crashed at Judge Proctor's?"

"One of them. Too many sightings for just one ship. Some of the witnesses strike me as self-promoting, like that astronomer fellow. Whiskey and pranks surely played a part. And the papers have never been averse to outright lies. But the one fellow I believed—" He breaks off in a coughing fit.

Ackerman sits in the other chair, his hands on his knees, waiting for August to finish.

"Rivers," August finishes.

"Nute Rivers? That old reprobate? He was one of the rabble-rousers that stirred up trouble for Nadine, you know. He's at odds with Pastor Allen now. Says the pastor has turned his back on God for supporting Nadine."

"He has his beliefs. Right or wrong, he's consistent." August sips the last of his sweet tea. "But I believed his airship story. The man's no liar."

"So, in the end, you got what you came to town for."

August blushes, putting some color in his face. "No." He laughs. "I'll tell you a secret. I was hoping to go for a ride in one of those things."

Ackerman slaps his thigh. "I believe you'd do just that." He sighs. "Oh, by the way. I heard something funny about ol' Russell Walters. I always wondered what happened to him that night. He and his employees were supposed to come out here and grab Nadine. Turns out only two showed up, so they decided to let the railroad boys go it alone. Three of the other employees came out here with us, so there's that. I guess two men at his side wasn't enough to risk getting shot."

"Just two showed, eh?"

Ackerman chuckles. "Two future foremen, I figure."

"I hope Walters has no steam left in his engine for bothering Nadine?"

"None." Ackerman taps the paper bag. "Brought you something else." He opens the bag and pulls out a bottle of medicine.

August nods. "My thanks. You go down to Fort Worth for that?"

The sly grin is back. "No, I didn't have to. Seems the town doctor had a change of heart. That'll happen when the pastor tells his congregation to get their doctoring done in Aurora." He puts the bottle of laudanum in August's lap. "This is from the doc's personal reserves, with his regards."

"How hard did you twist his arm?" August asks.

"Spun it like a whirligig."

They both chuckle and then sit without speaking. A fly buzzes around Ackerman's head and he waves it off. After a few minutes, August fumbles with the cork. Ackerman takes the bottle from him and hands it over. August takes a healthy swig and begins coughing. Ackerman closes his hands around August's to secure the bottle.

"Thank you," August says. "I'm struggling a bit."

"Nothing to apologize for." Ackerman sits back, a look of concern on his face. He pats August's knee. "Any regrets, August?"

"Too many to name."

Ackerman frowns. "Like what?"

August settles back into his chair. "During the war, I followed orders and sent men to their deaths."

"You're not alone in that," Ackerman says.

"Regrettably, no. But in view of recent events, I wonder at the point of it all. More than half a million people died to preserve the Republic and end the institution that blighted it. Yet we face the same maddening dilemmas." August scratches his chin and then sneaks his hand back under the blanket. "It seems to me now that life is a river, and people race downstream without paddles. If we're lucky, we learn to pitch our vessels from side to side, just enough to steer around the big rocks. And if we're *very* lucky, we enjoy the ride." He pauses. He can feel his throat tighten and his eyes water. "But the river keeps rolling, and those yet to come will face the same rocks, trapped in the same current. Nothing's better for my having been here."

"No such thing," Ackerman says, holding his thumb and index finger a half inch apart. "The world is a tiny bit better, and that's all you've a right to expect." He puts his hand back on August's knee. "Some fights are eternal. Men are not. You did your part, and you're allowed to pass the torch."

. . .

Night stretches ahead of him like a dark road. He marks time tracking a rectangle of moonlight from the window as it moves across his bedspread like the hour hand of a clock. The house creaks and pops as the day's heat slips away, but there are no other sounds. Everyone is asleep but August.

The laudanum does not make him sleepy tonight. His mind is ordered. He recalls each word of his conversation with Ackerman. *Some fights are eternal.* Had he not said much the same thing to Bose? Perhaps it was time to listen to himself. He is, after all, a wise man.

The thought makes him smile.

Lying motionless takes its toll. Various itches need scratching, and his legs begin to twitch under the covers. He wonders if he needs to urinate. He can't always tell anymore. At last, he throws back the covers and sits up. No dizziness. He stands and walks to the window.

In the distance, he sees the motte of trees. It seems closer at night. His eyes have always been sharper in the dark. Feeling clearheaded, he dresses. Sleep has eluded him and the bed is uncomfortable. He will go to the porch and sit. He wanders to the front of the house, bumping against a wall in the dark. When he reaches the kitchen, he lights Nadine's lantern and steps outside. The air is bracing, and his legs feel stronger than they have in days. He carries the lantern down the steps and stops.

The motte of trees is lit from behind. A steady light that does not flicker.

"By God," he whispers. An idea has come to him. "Why not?" He takes a few steps into the saw grass and stops, looking behind him. The house is quiet. He smiles and begins walking.

Why does he feel so energized? Perhaps the disease has receded. No, that can't be. It's more likely the large dose of laudanum has given him sails.

He steps lightly. There are holes and ridges in the ground, and he does not want to fall on his face. He is old. His bones are brittle. The lantern casts enough of a halo to avoid the obvious pitfalls. Ahead, the motte of trees seems as far away as before, though a glance tells him the house has been left well behind.

He recalls reading about his malady. When death is near, there is often a temporary remission of symptoms. Perhaps that is what he's feeling. The doctor in Rhome believed he'd have another six months, perhaps a year. That was three weeks ago. "Doctors," he says, chuckling. The lamp is light in his hand, and he feels as if he could walk forever.

And he may have to—the motte is still so far away. As he walks, he stares at the steady light behind the trees. No flicker. Is the source electric? His heart begins to speed up, whether from exertion or excitement. There is no reason to suspect that the light comes from an airship, but he begins to wonder. What other explanation?

His eyes on the stand of trees, he trips and begins to fall. He is careful with the lamp and not so careful with his head, bouncing face-first on the ground. Stunned, he lies flat, afraid to move.

The soil smells rich with a hint of sour. He tests his arms, then his legs, and discovers he has suffered no great damage. The lantern is likewise miraculously unharmed. He stands, brushes himself off, and picks the lantern up by its handle.

By the time he reaches the edge of the motte, the light behind the trees is much brighter. August weaves his way through the live oaks and cedar elms, his gaze locked on the greenish, phosphorescent glow. At last, he reaches a small clearing with an unimpeded view of the source.

The craft is seventy feet long, perhaps more. Cigar shaped. If it has windows, August can't see them—the light is blinding. It hovers without a sound, fifteen feet off the ground with no visible means of support. The air is charged with the fresh, pungent smell of an impending storm.

Heart pounding, August steps forward. He holds the lamp out, swinging it to the left and then the right. "Hello," he whispers.

The craft does not move.

August waits.

Then, moving in measured increments, the craft tilts left, then right.

August feels an indescribable sense of elation.

The craft tilts forward then. Not cigar shaped at all—he's been viewing it from the side. Tilted forward, he can see that the airship is saucer shaped.

Now the ship begins to rise, still soundless. The higher it goes, the more speed it attains, so that within seconds, it pierces the clouds. An afterglow lights the mist from above for just a moment, and then the sky is dark. The only light left hangs from a handle in his hands. He sets the lantern down.

"Well," he whispers. Suddenly tired—it was a very long walk, after all—he sits facing the clearing, his back to a tree. He can rest here. He listens to the night. No screech owls. No mockingbirds. Silence.

Then he hears the rustle of underbrush and soft footfalls.

The doe. No more than a dozen feet away. The animal regards him as if he were just another tree. He doesn't speak, for fear of scaring her, so it's a surprise when the deer says, "Hello."

August knows the voice. His heart does a flip in his chest, or perhaps he imagines that, too. "Was it you all along?" he asks.

The doe leans down for a nibble of greenery.

"Christy?"

The doe looks up. "I missed you," she says.

August considers this. "Deer can't talk," he says.

"And what do you deduce from that, my beloved?"

August smiles. "I suspect that my race is run."

The doe bows her head.

August takes a deep breath. He can smell soil and undergrowth—and fur.

He tries to stand but can't. He steels himself and tries again but is unable to rise. He looks to the doe and shrugs. "What now?" he asks.

The doe turns to go.

"Wait," August says. He tries again, and this time, he stands without effort, suddenly free of what held him to the ground. He is light as dew. Light as a dream.

"Come with me," the doe says, looking back. "It's time for your next adventure."

AFTER

Early in the morning, an hour before the sun rises, Nadine steps out on the porch for a moment alone before the day's work begins. The air won't be this cool for the rest of the day and she craves the silence. The moon is down, though the stars are still out. In the distance, she sees a pinprick of light from a lantern, which leads her to August's body.

Because of the heat, August is buried in Aurora the following day, next to his beloved Christy. August made the arrangements in advance. Though Bill tells everyone that his friend had wanted a private burial, a number of townspeople come to say goodbye, including Bose, Abigail, and Mr. Hanson. Pastor Allen, who'd moved back into the boarding house, rides in the buckboard to the service with Nadine, Natalie, MacGregor, and William Chambers.

The sandstone sculpture with Bullet's attempted likeness is placed at the head of August's grave. When the kind words and tears are over, Ackerman tosses a few metal nuggets on top of the simple wood casket, along with the first handful of dirt.

The sandstone carving sparks some discussion, due to its unconventional nature. Ackerman refuses to explain the strange carving, and some townspeople speculate that the markings on the face are a representation of the airship. The eyes and nostril are clearly windows. August was, admittedly, a strange man, so most don't give the idiosyncratic marker a second thought.

As promised, a check arrives from August's solicitor. When Nadine receives it, she bursts into tears and spends much of the afternoon in her bedroom, weeping. After consulting with Abigail, she walks the field with her daughter Natalie. She explains what August has done, and what it means, and Natalie bursts into tears as well, for she will be going away to college after all.

Repairs on the boarding house are made. Though Bill Ackerman avoids physical work, he performs well as a supervisor, directing repairs and the delivery of materials, ensuring that Nadine and Abigail are not cheated. In his new capacity, Ackerman becomes a frequent visitor to the boarding house, usually arriving in time for the service of a meal.

The following spring, the country's attention focuses on Cuba. An American warship, the *USS Maine,* explodes in Havana Harbor, and newspapers published by Hearst and Pulitzer blame Spain. The relentless demand for action overwhelms President McKinley's call for patience. In April, the United States declares war on Spain.

Three years later, McKinley is shot dead by an anarchist who viewed McKinley as a symbol of oppression.

From China, a third great historical pandemic—the Hong Kong Plague—wreaks havoc, carried aboard ships to ports across the world on flea-infested rats. By the time the disease runs its course, more than fifteen million people will have died.

In Rhome, life proceeds much as it has for generations. The townspeople worship at two separate Methodist churches—one for blacks and one for whites. The men from the mills grind wheat during the day and drink at Hanson's in the evening. Farmers plant their crops. Women sweep Texas dirt from their porches. Babies are born. The dead are buried to the sound of hymns and weeping. The town survives.

And at the end of April, when soft rains and the smell of soil remind him of springs past, and the painted buntings and cattle egrets sing their songs of renewal, Bill Ackerman changes his mind and buys another horse.

AUTHOR'S NOTE

The airship mystery—the backdrop for this novel—occurred much as I presented it, though August's conclusions (and mine) about what really happened are conjecture. For a month in 1897, Texas newspapers reported hundreds of UFO sightings, seven years before the Wright brothers flew at Kitty Hawk.

News then—as now—had a shelf life. The airship mystery was very nearly forgotten until 1973, when Bill Case, aviation writer for the *Dallas Times Herald*, published an article on the "Texas Roswell." Case also served as the state director of the Mutual UFO Network (MUFON). As part of the investigation, a gravesite in the Aurora cemetery was examined. The headstone appeared to have a spacecraft carved into the face. Metal detectors indicated traces of metal in the grave itself. Case asked for permission to exhume the grave, but the city of Aurora refused.

Later, the sandstone marker in question was stolen, making it impossible to determine exactly which grave should be examined. Cemetery records indicated that the area in question was in use between 1880 and 1900. Because the remains of the suspected alien could have been buried in one of several locations, further requests for exhumation were denied. In lieu of digging, researchers used ground-penetrating radar, but the results were inconclusive.

The site of the Proctor farm was explored as well, including the old well. There, more metal bits were found. When analyzed, they included shards of aluminum along with nuggets composed of an "unidentified metal element."

ACKNOWLEDGEMENTS

One of my life's blessings is membership in two different critique groups. The members—all excellent writers—spot errors and let me know when I've jumped the literary shark. Thanks go to Patricia Stoltey, Kenneth Harmon, Gordon MacKinney, Brigitte Dempsey, Jim Davidson, and Laura Mahal of the Raintree Writers. Also, Aaron Spriggs, Jim Norris, Tarra Hartman, Jeff Bibbey, Chris Pimental, and Mimi Wahlfeldt of the Penpointers.

Special thanks to Laura Mahal, who edited the final manuscript. Laura, who is an outstanding wordsmith, went as far as to utilize a turn-of-the-century dictionary while fine-tuning my novel. You might have spotted odd phrasing or spelling, some of which happened in service of authenticity.

Finally, thanks (as always) to Judith, a lover of good books, published poet, and the most supportive wife a man could have.

Anyone wishing to correspond with me about this novel can reach me via email at brian@nunntelwb.com.

Brian Kaufman
December 2022

ABOUT THE AUTHOR

A Persistent Echo is Brian Kaufman's eighth published novel. He lives in the Colorado mountains with his wife Judith and his dog Finn. In his spare time, he lifts weights, plays blues guitar, and keeps local microbreweries in business with his bad behavior.

OTHER TITLES BY BRIAN KAUFMAN

"... successfully melds historical fiction and horror ...
... a moody pastoral tale with a creepy paranormal conclusion."
—*Indie Reader*

BRIAN KAUFMAN

A SHADOW MELODY

NOTE FROM BRIAN KAUFMAN

Word-of-mouth is crucial for any author to succeed. If you enjoyed *A Persistent Echo*, please leave a review online—anywhere you are able. Even if it's just a sentence or two. It would make all the difference and would be very much appreciated.

Thanks!
Brian Kaufman

We hope you enjoyed reading this title from:

www.blackrosewriting.com

Subscribe to our mailing list – *The Rosevine* – and receive **FREE** books, daily deals, and stay current with news about upcoming releases and our hottest authors.
Scan the QR code below to sign up.

Already a subscriber? Please accept a sincere thank you for being a fan of Black Rose Writing authors.

View other Black Rose Writing titles at
www.blackrosewriting.com/books and use promo code
PRINT to receive a **20% discount** when purchasing.

CPSIA information can be obtained
at www.ICGtesting.com
Printed in the USA
BVHW040525180323
660291BV00001B/1

9 781685 132682